THE
UPRIGHT
HEART

THE UPRIGHT HEART

A NOVEL

JULIA AIN-KRUPA

New Europe Books

Williamstown, Massachusetts

Published by New Europe Books, 2016
Williamstown, Massachusetts
www.NewEuropeBooks.com
Copyright © Julia Ain-Krupa, 2016
Cover design by Oksana Shmygol
Cover photo by Vladimir Korostyshevskiy
Interior design by Knowledge Publishing Services

ISBN: 978-0-9900043-8-7

Cataloging-in-Publication Data is available from the Library of Congress.

First English-language edition

10 9 8 7 6 5 4 3 2 1

Acknowledgments

This book would never have been made possible without the generous grant awarded me by the Fulbright Commission, which originally took me to Krakow in 2012.

Life, laughter, love, and work would not be possible without my friends and family in Krakow, New York, and now also in Tel Aviv. You all make it possible for me to soar. To my Dotan and his friends, to Mara, to Alice and Teresa, to Lyn and Will, to Denise, Paulina, Marin, Anna, Asia, Esther, Verushka, Danae, Katie, Tala, Adel, Antosia, Samara, Liana, Alex, Alexis, Wendy, and countless others. There is no room in this world to express what you all mean to me. You make the world home.

Thank you to Jonathan Ornstein and Kasia Leonardi, who helped make Krakow my new home. Thank you to Rabbi Avi Baumol for his patience and interest in all my questioning. To my fellow Fulbrighters and writers, Denise Grollmus and Oksana Lutsyshyna, who encouraged me through the first pages of this book, and who held my hand during that first Polish winter. To the invaluable Joanna Sliwa, to Dara Bramson and Dara Weinberg, to survivors Sofia Radzikowska and Henryk Meller, and to Pan Mundek Elbinger, Pan Gamon, and Bernard Kuśka. Thank you to Slawek Pastuszek and the entire community of the Krakow JCC. To Malgosia Ploszaj and to all those Poles I have met who devote themselves to preserving Jewish culture and heritage in Poland, with no personal gain or reward but simply because they feel an absence and are moved to do something. Certain places and memories stand out for me, including the Jewish community of Lublin, and traveling with Justyna to the forests near Bialystok, where graves were overgrown with vines and little red berries grew wild.

Scott Morgan, Elspeth Treadwell, Andrew Seear, Tana Ross, Leah Rhodes, Didi Drachman, Deborah Kearns, Anne Thulin, Fred Pirkey, Randy Bloom, Zahra Partovi and Vincent Fitzgerald, Judy and Michael Sacks, Catherine Shainberg, Beth Biegler, and Kathleen Farrell.

Antosia Kondrat and her family, Olga, Janusz, and Marysia Stoklosa, Franek Mula, Esther, Nili, and Natty de R, the Mulji family, Gabi and Uwe Von Seltmann, Olga and Ania Szwajger, Teatr Stu, Muriel Shockley, Lisa Wells, Joanna Anderson, Maria Makuch, and the people who always encouraged me to write, especially Elysha Schneider, Zowie Broach, and Brian Kirkby.

Thank you for the help of Anna Spysz, Robert Braille, Elzbieta Mankowska, Dorota Nowak, and William Vidal, and historians Edyta Gawron, Tomek Jankowski, Anna Pero, Grzegorz Jezowski, and Katarzyna Zimmerer.

Thank you to my patient and kind publisher, Paul Olchváry, at New Europe Books, and to my cover designer, Oksana Shmygol, whose angelic spirit and beautiful design work helped make this book what I dreamt it to be.

For the cafés that serviced my imagination, especially Bliekle, in Krakow, and Cheder. To the New York Society Library's beautiful writer's room, which has provided me with a makeshift office for the past four years.

Thank you to Dotan. Your entrance into my life is a long-awaited blessing. Thank you for your incredible love and for being so uniquely you. I love you more every day.

And, finally, thank you to Krakow, my eternal home, with its beautiful cobblestone streets, its mist-filled air, and its loving people who have always made me feel that I too can belong.

For my ancestors, who took me by the hand,
Dorothy Ain, Wolf Ain, Viktor Frieholc,
and Elzbieta Krupa.

For my parents,
Noa Ain and Olek Krupa

For rabbi Boaz Pash, who,
though he was afraid of my questions,
allowed me to ask them anyway.

And for those who passed away
while I was writing this book.
For Deborah Jacobson, Ryo Murakami,
Elzbieta Krupa, and Jonathan Ain.

Part I
The Exodus

We are all called Sarah. My name used to be Rachelka, but then it was changed, and now I am Sarah just like all the other girls. My house is built of fragile bones. They shine like crystal prayers in the moonlight. Breathing with the rest of the world, they tremble with mystery and become mirror images of that last living thing that gives us life, the night. These bones are built of the same calcium that once belonged to the stars. At least that is what Pan Kubilak taught us in science class, and I can never forget it.

And what are we now? Are we still living, trapped inside this old house with no visible walls, only bones to support a transparent roof? Are we like the house? Does an undetectable presence within us marvel at the beauty of our remains as they shine in the brilliant night? We cannot step beyond these invisible walls, and yet we wonder, after so much time, is there really anywhere to go? And where would forty-one Sarahs go to make a new home, anyway?

I

Wiktor Frieholtz is running late again. He awakes this morning to a strange aching in his head, a burning sensation in his stomach. Not wanting to go to work, he retreats beneath the warm coziness of his duvet cover and tries to hide from his wife, Waleria, for as long as he can without being noticed. Praying for invisibility, he caresses the lace trim of his blanket with his toes. *My wife made this,* he tells himself, and examines the outline of his hands, which are so closely connected to those of his wife after so many years of marriage. He knows that she will come into the room and yell at him (with maternal kindness, of course). He knows that he will get up and go, running as always, but for this moment in time he claims total ignorance. He peeks from beneath the covers as a child would, absorbing the first signs of spring as they cast shadows on the newly painted wall. The war has been over for a year. Life begins again.

When her shouting becomes unbearable, he dresses and shaves before the old brass mirror. Wiktor always shaves, even when he is late. He runs his hand across his closely cropped hair and touches the cross that hangs humbly over the doorframe, as he always does, even on mornings like this. He takes a sip of coffee and in three bites eats his morning bread and butter, while almost simultaneously kissing his daughter, Elżbieta, her newborn son, Mateusz, and his wife on the head. Before they know it he is out the door.

"Wiktor Frieholtz is running late again," Pani Ewa says as she removes a saucer of milk from the stove for her husband's morning coffee and catches a glimpse of his back as he brushes the branches of her rose bush, its tiny buds bursting at the seams. Traces of his silhouette linger in the patterned lace curtain that shelters her kitchen from the outside world.

Wiktor is running late, but he is almost there.

Adjusting the knot on his tie, he passes Pan Buchta's yard, where a group of drunken soldiers nearly blasted all the fine tomato plants away for good last year. Small vines retrace their paths, remembering with pride where they once did reside. Wiktor notices Pan Buchta's bent figure like the classic representation of an old crone, his hand as it rustles through newly turned soil, but by the time Pan Buchta is able to look up and see him, he is already gone.

Past the Makowski twins, who are arguing over who will get to carry the wounded sparrow, and through the brush, across the little bridge and into the fields that every morning carry Wiktor to work and that at the end of every day bring him home. It wasn't long ago that soldiers were camped here, along this very stream. Its banks were their tiny trenches, and when the war came to a close, they left behind their helmets, their bayonets, what little treasures the neighborhood children could collect and trade, and headed straight for a nonexistent home. Now these stream banks are all free land. The only permanent inhabitants are rabbits and squirrels. *As it should be,* Wiktor whispers to himself while climbing the hill to the train tracks where he works. The air is fresh and smells of wild thyme and hay, and Wiktor has the idea that spring exists for the first time. After a lifetime of winter, of war, Wiktor cannot help but smile at the awakening

Wiktor has no chance to check in with the train dispatcher, and having just buttoned his jacket and tied his tie, he gingerly removes his jacket, rolls up the cuffs of his white starched shirt, and begins to work. His newly cut hair whistles in the wind, but he has no time to pay attention to the sound. He crouches before the tracks, checking the switch that enables trains to change paths as they approach the station. The local train is headed his way as he busies himself with an old rusty track. In fact he is so busy with his work that he does not notice the wind as it changes directions, does not hear the train approaching, does not see it barreling down. There is a tremendous sound. He does not realize that it is the sound of his own blood boiling, his own mind racing, as his body is being crushed.

Mid-breath now. Is there an exhale that takes place up in the sky? Out in the ether, Wiktor, did you watch how we cried? How people came all the way from Katowice to mourn your loss? How

Waleria locked herself in her room, cross in hand, berating herself for letting you go? How she held her baby grandson in her arms and cried that he was a gift from God? Did you see us weeping when the doorbell rang every day at five and there was no one waiting to be let inside? For weeks the bell rang, but still you were never there. We knew you were gone, but we waited for you anyway. Did you take one last breath before you took flight?

Wiktor rises from beneath the weight of the steel train, now resting like a feather on his new form. He walks slowly, sensing every atom of his movement as he never has before. He does not look behind. He does not see the wreckage of his body, but rather moves with some kind of childlike delight. Each step feels like a gentle transition in space, the thrill of each molecule of matter spurring him on, as if his body has no separation from the earth or the sky. *Must be the headiness of spring,* he tells himself. But even spring cannot induce such exaltation. He thinks better of what has happened, recalling that morning and the feeling in his stomach that told him not to go. He thinks of Waleria's hands. Suddenly frightened by his weightlessness, Wiktor looks down at his hands for reassurance of his existence, but there is nothing there. He discovers now that he has no hands, only space where dexterity lived just moments ago.

He cannot move quickly, and there is no way to go home. There is only one movement, only one direction in which to go.

II

Wiktor returns to the banks of the stream, and daylight has dimmed as if it is already evening and morning light is turning to night. The smoke from Rybnik's coal-burning stoves blows across the stream, and Wiktor strains to see. He notices a strange lump on the ground and bends down to find a muddy helmet obstructing his path. Not far away lies a pile of bayonets, which leads him to a group of German soldiers sitting by the river. In silence they look out over the stream. One man with broad shoulders and features so identifiably unlike that of a Pole smokes a hand-rolled cigarette, flicking the ashes into the slow-moving current. His cheeks are ruddy from too many nights spent out in the cold, and his shirt is torn across the chest. There are patches of snow where the men are sitting. Winter is in their hearts as they wait for something to change. Wiktor walks up to the smoking man and nods a hello.

"Is it winter now?" Wiktor asks, squatting beside the German.

The young soldier turns to him slowly, his eyes glassy and pale as if his vision is obfuscated by the world. He looks at Wiktor's tiny frame and shrugs his shoulders as if he could care less what time of year it is. He wipes his nose with the back of his sleeve and looks off toward a distant field.

"Who knows?" the man mumbles. "It is always winter now. We've been waiting for days and days and nothing. No one has come to get us. No one has told us who is winning. Who cares if it's winter? We might as well be dead."

Wiktor swallows.

"He's right!" chimes in another soldier, gaunt and tired as he leans his baby face against his pack, the heels of his boots digging into the fresh, snowy mud. He laughs hysterically and caresses his groin as if looking for comfort.

A gentle moan is emitted from the group as a soldier of about eighteen stands above the rest and begins to shout, his legs trembling, spit forming at the corners of his mouth.

"I keep asking, why don't we do something!" he cries. "I cannot continue to sit by this river without knowing what is happening! I need to know! Captain, please! I keep thinking about my mother sitting at the kitchen table waiting for a letter. She isn't moving. She isn't eating or sleeping. She is in a warm house but she is worse off than we are. Please! She is just waiting! Please help us to find out what is happening! Help us to get home." His eyes are pleading as he looks to the smoking man, who blows perfectly formed smoke rings that mingle with the foggy air. He barely flinches an eye.

"Upon your order, captain," he mumbles, shrinking back into a seated position.

"I can tell you," Wiktor whispers.

He clears his throat and begins again. He wonders why his voice is quivering when he feels so calm. "I can help you find a way to get home."

III

It is dinnertime in all the houses on Strzelecka Street except one. Here, nobody has the will to cook. They eat bread and butter. They don't wash the dishes. They do what they can to get through the day. Elżbieta is living in a dream in which the world is distant and alive. She can taste, see, and smell the dust molecules in the air. She asks herself, *Is this what death brings?* The atmosphere is humming.

On the wall to the left that separates this room from the next is a layer of paint so fresh that the paintings meant to hang there are placed carefully on the floor. It wasn't long ago that this wall was no more than a gaping hole. It wasn't long ago that soldiers took Elżbieta and her family from their house at gunpoint.

"Just shoot!" Elżbieta's sister Henia shouted. Elżbieta shook at the invitation.

When the family was finally allowed to return to their home, Wiktor spent every Sunday evening carefully repairing the wall and reconstructing their world. He had just finished applying the second coat of paint.

Elżbieta takes Mateusz from her mother's arms and rocks him to sleep. *"Aaa, kotki dwa,"* she sings. *There are two cats.* Lullabies emerge from the recesses of her memory when holding her baby in her arms. It is as if they went to sleep somewhere in the back of her mind, and waited for that moment when they would offer shelter to another human being. Motherhood is new to Elżbieta. So is orphanhood.

There is nothing but this baby to hold me down, she thinks. *If it weren't for this little baby and his unquenchable thirst, I would surely fly away. I would rise up into the sky and I would meet you there. How many years will it be before I see you again, Papa?*

She rests her feet on a little stool as she switches the baby from her right breast to her left. She stares at the westward wall of the room and through the windows that look out over the garden and surrounding fields. She rocks herself gently. The sun is misty and pink, as if peering down on their little town through a lens of clouded glass. In this region of Poland daylight can seem like a pale and hallucinatory dream, so white that it is as if God were trying to erase the world.

Through the open window Elżbieta can hear the sound of eager raindrops even though there is no rain. They hit the tender grass, patches of brown and green moss so soft that they seem to belong to a fairytale much more than they do the streets of a coalmining town. The trees are swiftly shedding frost accumulated overnight. To the right is a stream that has set the stage for so many events in her life, and beyond are the train tracks where her father was killed. As far as the eye can see looking west, there are only fields and forests beyond. Other than the sound of the drops as they fall, everything is so quiet. There is only the bubble of rain and the sound of her heart beating, racing inside her head, but there is nowhere for her to run.

At this moment, those worries that have always tugged at the back of her mind begin to surface. Elżbieta thinks of her little brother, Karol, now in kindergarten, now without a father. Will he live to fight in another war? Or, like their father, will he live to see another war through, only to die needlessly once it is over? Will he get picked on in school for being so small? What time is it? Will he make it safely home? She hopes the front door is locked, so that they are all safe, so that her baby is safe. Is it locked? She cannot remember. And then she repeats the questions to herself, for they sound like a comforting song.

Elżbieta's mother comes into the room and sits beside her.

"Oh Mama," Elżbieta cries, and buries her face in her mother's chest. The baby awakes and begins to wail. Elżbieta rocks him to sleep. There is only silence. Even the little rain has come to an end.

IV

Wiktor has decided to take the soldiers over the bridge and into town. The smoking man is quiet, but the younger members of the group are enthusiastic about leaving the banks of the river behind. The group moves slowly, six tall men following one smaller Wiktor. The soldiers take care not to slip as their boots meet the warm ground and the snow melts away. Only the beetles can hear their sound.

The smoke from the coal mines mingles with the foggy night air, and it is so dark that Wiktor becomes unmoored at moments, as if he cannot remember which way to go. He is careful not to reveal this uncertainty.

On their way into town the group takes Strzelecka Street, and soon passes Wiktor's house. The front gate is locked, but the lights are on upstairs, and Wiktor can see Waleria and Elżbieta sitting and talking. He wants to wave to them, but then remembers that he has no hands.

In my empty heart, in the space where it once was, I am waving to you. I am sending you my love.

The night has settled in, and as they walk down the hill, past the church, there is no one around.

"It is so quiet," the youngest, baby-faced soldier whispers to no one in particular, fumbling with the small, star-shaped gold pin dangling from the lapel of his jacket.

"I say we go for a drink," the smoking captain, who is the commanding officer, snarls as they pass a small bar at the edge of town. Inside, men are sitting at small wooden tables somberly drinking vodka. The only woman present is a short, middle-aged barmaid.

"No. No drinks," Wiktor says quietly. Despite his hushed voice, he is still heard.

"There is someone that I would like to stop and see, if you don't mind," says the gaunt, slow-moving soldier, gesturing toward Wiktor, standing close behind him but never looking him in the eye. "A girl."

"It won't work," Wiktor says, turning to the young man. "I'm sorry, but it just won't. Besides, we don't have time. We have somewhere to go."

"I don't know why you say it won't work. It works just fine. . . ."

There is the sound of a dog barking, and as is always true in Rybnik, when one dog barks, all the other dogs must chime in, and so a chorus of singing dogs resounds through the streets.

"Funny," the first young soldier remarks. "Everything sounds so far away."

"Left here," Wiktor commands, as he takes the group around the side of the town's old church.

The barking dog wanders around the corner and saunters directly toward them, exhaling clouds of wet fog into the soft brown light of a nearby street lamp. From behind the German shepherd emerges a young couple, arms locked as they walk. They gaze at one another, just as people do in spring after war. Her hair is golden, and her coat is made of felt wool, burning bright red in the dark night. She is a beacon of light. She walks toward the young soldier, the gaunt one, as he stops moving and whispers her name, "Zosia." She walks briskly past him, as if he wasn't there at all.

Zosia pulls her coat tightly closed and leans in to her lover. "It is chilly tonight, isn't it?" she asks, a shiver crawling up her spine. Her lover simply looks down at her and smiles as they walk off into the dark night.

The gaunt soldier shakes as he follows the group out of the light.

Wiktor leads the men to a door at the back of the church. This is the crypt, he wants to tell them, but he doesn't have the heart to say the word. The men have hopeful faces. The steps leading down are dark and damp, but the men can only perceive the cold. They shudder because they know they should.

Being alive was like riding a boat and letting the waves knock you around until you could barely orient yourself to the world, the youngest soldier thinks quietly, not wanting anyone else to hear. It is all over now. It is all over. It is. Darkness enshrouds the group. Not even a footstep or the echo of footsteps can be heard.

V

They call it a nebula. What lights up the night sky in an explosion of blue, red, orange, green. Colors you don't know about yet. Colors you've never seen.

I know that there is a buzz in the heart that lingers long after you are gone. I know that it lifts you up, out of your body and higher until you are in the beyond. I am suspended here, above the nebula, in this ring of planets, and I cannot even remember where I come from or what came before. I can only remember a sound and maybe a feeling. I can recall needing someone once, I think.

We are one system, this ring of tiny planets, this white feather and me. If I look back and try to remember, if I drop, the feather rises. If the feather falls, I float up.

What is the measure of a heart? The weight of a feather, you might say.

I am waiting to begin again.

VI

Wiktor and his group of soldiers make their way into the crypt of the Rybnik town church. The church spire extends toward the sky and can be seen from everywhere in town, a reminder that God is watching. There is a row of tombs on each side of the passageway, and the smell of mold hangs heavy in the air, but the group remains oblivious to it.

"What exactly are we doing here?" the captain asks Wiktor, leaning against the cold stone wall. He might as well be standing in a bar holding a beer and talking to a girl.

"There are tunnels that lead somewhere behind one of these doors."

"But where will they take us?" the young, gaunt soldier asks, his pale face haunting in the dim, basement light. He looks longingly into Wiktor's smiling dark eyes. "She didn't even see me," he whispers. "She didn't even say hello."

"No, she didn't," Wiktor replies, looking away. He turns back to their leader.

"I know that these tunnels were used during the resistance. They go to Kraków, to Warsaw, maybe even to Berlin."

"They will lead us nowhere," one soldier says. "Is the war over?"

"It is. I am not certain where these tunnels lead, but you must try," Wiktor replies. "There is a chance they will take you home."

The captain nods and the group moves carefully past the tombs of priests and of local saints. There is a wooden door at the end of the corridor that opens to a dusty tunnel. Wiktor takes the soldiers through. He stands at attention.

"I must leave you all here," he says. "Let you continue on your own."

"Thank you," the captain replies, and Wiktor turns to leave. "Thank you for helping us get home. Maybe we will see each other again."

"You will be just fine if you follow the tunnels. Your mothers and your wives are waiting for you."

"But wait," the young soldier says, turning toward Wiktor. "Please tell us, who won?"

Wiktor turns his back and says nothing as he retraces his steps and walks past them, out of the crypt. They are transfixed.

The captain bends down to examine something colorful on the ground.

"What is it?" the gaunt soldier asks, taking a step back.

"A flower," the captain replies. "Growing here, in the dark."

VII

Is it any good that we all share a name? Yes, it is. This way we can remind each other who we are whenever we forget. I am Sarah and so is she. We all wear the same uniforms and play the same games. Only now the games we play are different than before.

The Łódź girl's school was our haven in life and it is for us now as well. All of our classmates were Jewish except for four Polish girls. We all had things in common. All of us had refined clothing, a warm home to return to, and parents who could afford to give us a good education. Not only could they give it, but they also wanted their daughters to have it. Where are those four Polish girls now? Eating dinner somewhere in the countryside, perhaps? Still recovering from the war? They are Magdalena, Małgosia, Malwina, and Anna.

We are left behind. We sit at our desks, dressed in uniform, making lace figurines out of water and light. We catch the slightest specks of matter and then we weave them into something beautiful.

Daisy, Daisy
Give me your answer, do.
I'm half crazy
All for the love of you.

This is the chorus of Sarah's favorite song. She learned it from an American musical that once played for three weeks in a row at the town cinema before the war. She snuck out to see it seven times and spent every night for months trying to learn to dance the way the lead girl did in the movie. Her name was Gingerogers, I think. Whenever we get sad or lonely Sarah tells us to stand in a circle and sing this song until we can't sing it any more. She knows how to get us going, and sometimes she can even make us laugh. That is her gift. She would have made a wonderful actress or comedian. Besides, she is very beautiful.

We like playing games. We do lessons sometimes as well, examining our old botany books, or even studying geography, which was a favorite subject for many of us. We used to dream together of all the places in the world we would one day go. Many of the girls wanted to go to Hawaii, but I have always dreamt of one day seeing the great mountains of Peru.

With our knowledge of astronomy we can sometimes locate the constellations through the roof of our broken home. This is another one of our favorite activities, especially little Sarah's. She was only nine when we died, and so had less time to learn and to love. Often she becomes angry and doesn't want to participate or agree to anything, but we must be patient. Her time was even shorter than ours.

When she is inconsolable, I take her by the hand and lead her to the grand hallway that looks out over the road where factory smoke billows in the distance. Łódź is filled with factories, many of which were opened by our relatives. The sky is vibrant here, and I try to teach her the names of all the constellations: Andromeda, Cassiopeia. Every so often she dares to crack a smile.

"Will it always be this way?" she asks, her eyes still wet with expectation, even long after the answer has been found.

"No it won't," I tell her, looking into her eyes, trying to reassure her and maybe even myself. "It won't always be this way, but I don't know how or when it will change." We are waiting for someone to come and unlock the gate.

Nobody knows for sure just when we will be allowed to leave this home and move on to the next.

Sarah, whose grandfather was a great rabbi, says we are caught between worlds because we died too fast and did not complete our tikkun. Sarah is the one we always turn to when we have important questions. Her name used to be Irina, which is a Russian name. Her mother was a Jewess who fell for her father one night in Petersburg. He was a traveling salesman, and was so taken by her mother's beauty that he laid his most beautiful Persian rug at her doorstep as a sign of his devotion.

Sometimes when the moon is full and we feel most at peace, Sarah tells us stories her grandfather once told her. She says that maybe, since we died so soon, we will return and live again. Maybe, Sarah says. This is all we know. We love our books and our stories. They are our tradition, our history. They may not be much, but they are what we still have. After all, we are only thirteen years old.

VIII

This night is quiet. All the dogs have gone to bed.

Wiktor is running again. Out of the crypt, past the church where he crossed the threshold with his wife on their wedding day, where his three children were baptized, where people came to mourn when he died.

Elżbieta is leaning against the kitchen table on Strzelecka Street, crushing rose petals and sugar with a spoon. The roses are freshly picked, as they always are in spring, still wet from the morning dew. It is almost midnight now, but she is still standing, trying her best to hold up the world. Making jam is a sign that home still exists, and so she turns the petals in a rhythmic motion, releasing their perfume into the night air that wafts from the cracked window into the room. Spring is on the tip of nature's tongue, and for a moment there is harmony. In one breath, life persists. As rose petals transform into a paste that will later become the jam of the gods, Elżbieta looks out the kitchen window onto the fields and scans the distant skyline, so soft that it is almost like a painting whose edges have been blurred by the addition of a splash of water. *Somewhere Papa is still running,* she thinks with a smile. *He is out there, up in heaven, now entering through those glistening gates.*

You see that star down there? It explodes every seven days or so. It gathers its strength for a little while, and then day after day it grows brighter until it bursts forth with the intensity of its own energy. I watch how it grows, how it catches remnants of the passing sun and competes with other stars for ultimate glory. You win, we all want to say, and oh how we laugh. Nobody cares up here about who is strongest, because here everybody is strong, even my little feather, who flies higher than all the rest.

IX

This is the night that Wiktor says goodbye to Rybnik, his hometown.

Ulica Strzelecka, goodbye. Town square, goodbye. River that runs, goodbye. Goodbye to all of the places and people I have loved.

Tiny newborn flowers are sprouting from the ground. They are deep red, pale violet, yellow, white. *The colors of my childhood, the colors of my life.* Green. And, of course, gray, the color of the Rybnik skyline.

Wiktor runs back toward the train tracks without knowing why. He sees the fields where he lived his entire life and they fill him with the memory of profound joy.

No more maybes. There is always a light shining somewhere beyond.

X

Wolf Ain is sitting at the window of wagon number four on the night train to Białystok, watching an endless stretch of darkness rush past. Just hours ago he was traveling through Austria. Now he is passing through Katowice on his way to Warsaw, and he will then go further east. This night is long as the train moves across the Polish landscape. If it were daylight he would see passing fields—humble, soft, endless green. A house in the distance where there is always a chimney smoking, even in summertime. Little red berries along the tracks, nettles pert and ready to prick any animal that dares approach; shadows, branches, and forests filled with the last traces of snow. But night shrouds the country in darkness. Wolf counts the occasional lamppost and chimney. Everything is silent other than the sound of the train rumbling over the tracks. It is that feeling of being cradled that rocks him to sleep, that sensation which brings him back to the first months of life, when there was always someone to hold him in her arms.

Wolf twirls a pink string given to him by baby Leah around his left fingers and tries to remember the Polish word for "spirit." In Russian it is *dusha*, and in Hebrew, *ruach*, like the wind. In Polish, it is *dusza.* This language is so difficult to learn but even harder to forget. Wolf plays with languages the way other people play with cards.

What kind of person would I be if I didn't go back to see? He asks himself, nodding off as the surrounding scenery fades into the background. The train lulls Wolf slowly to sleep, and his glasses slide down to the tip of his nose, so they might easily fall and shatter, but never do they let go.

XI

Running beside a train, you would normally feel the strength of steel as it barrels across the land. You would know your vulnerability, and would sense, suddenly, the fragility of your body as it pales in comparison to a great machine, to a product of man's imagination and not a figment of nature. But without a solid body, things are different, and running beside steel is no different than running beside a stream. You are like water, the steel is like a chariot waiting to take you in its arms. You can swim together. In fact, you could just as easily unite with the whole world. It is almost like flying. Wiktor feels that ecstasy as he leaps aboard the local train to Katowice. Not even a thought is needed to make it happen. Just the slightest intention, and he is already there.

Wolf's reflexes are fast enough to catch his eyeglasses before they fall to the floor of wagon number four, but it takes him longer to come to terms with his surroundings, and for a time he still hears a baby crying, still sees delicate pine needles pricking at his peripheral vision, as if his dream does not yet want to release him back into reality. The first signs of pink are appearing along the horizon in prelude to the dawn.

Having taken the leap from the fields that surround Rybnik onto the train, and then swiftly jumping to the Białystok train as it passes through Katowice, Wiktor walks through the corridor of wagon number four looking for the one who is calling him. Wiktor recognizes him immediately. Though he isn't wearing his kippah, he still looks like a stranger. (Not wearing a kippah is the one concession he felt he had to make in returning to Poland—that and leaving his tefillin and his tzitzit at home. This decision came after a big internal debate, though he felt he was making the right decision in the end.) Alone in the darkened car, Wolf sits below a small brown leather bag placed on the metal rack above his head. His dark beard is thick, and his wavy hair is carefully parted. He wears a lightweight brown woolen suit and a starched collared shirt. There is a discreet tear on the pocket of his shirt, barely visible as he leans against the window, asleep. He flinches, grabbing his glasses before they fall to the floor. Wolf's eyes open in a blurry manner that reminds Wiktor of his grandson, Mateusz, who always grins absentmindedly while drifting off to sleep. Wolf smiles in the direction of the open train car door, and Wiktor smiles, too, feeling for a moment that he is being seen. Wolf rallies himself and returns to gazing out the window at the last vestige of the night and the passing fields. He questions the world that streams before him. *Now I know,* he thinks. *Now I know that whatever you are away from feels like a dream.*

Wiktor comes to sit beside Wolf on the lumpy old bench. Just as it was with the soldiers in Rybnik, he feels compelled to be here with this man.

Now Rybnik is behind him. Now Rybnik is everywhere.

Wolf looks out the window, and Wiktor watches Wolf. The world drifts away as night gives way to dawn and heartbreak, their backs turned toward the future.

XII

There are three faded photographs stuffed into Wolf's suit coat pocket. No handkerchief, no dash of color, only three small crumpled photos to commemorate a life that has already split in two. The still, serious faces scattered across paper, the family posing in a dark parlor, backs upright, gazes still. From the torn lining of Wolf's coat, decorated with faded representations of European landmarks such as the Eiffel Tower and the Leaning Tower of Pisa, to the papers tucked into his breast pocket, nothing is hidden from Wiktor anymore.

Wolf twirls a little pink string around his pinky finger. The string was given to him by his daughter, Leah. She is the spitting image of his sister, also Leah, who used the Yiddish spelling of the same name, Leye. He gazes out the window and wonders just how long it has been since he has seen these forests of endless white birch, like fragile ghosts standing, shivering imperceptibly in the silent wind. And the beautiful poplar trees, the upright *topole* so characteristic of his childhood. He remembers when he was studying at Slobodka Yeshiva in Lithuania, how he looked to those trees as an embodiment of the kind of man he wanted to become, proud and unmovable. *Every time I travel home I will look to them as a marker of who I am becoming,* he would tell himself late at night as he was falling asleep, face in a book, night giving way to the dawn. Then, early in the morning, he would take a long walk in the forest, turning over the latest ethical question in his mind. *If I feel at one with that tree*—he would say to himself, pointing to the tallest and most alone of the scattered group—*then I will know that I am growing in the right way. Only then can I return home and call myself a man.*

If only I had known. If only I had known what kind of wind was about to blow.

When we left Poland I held on to that image. I am strong inside, I told myself. I know what it is to be a moral person in this world. It may have broken my heart to make the choices that I made, but at least it did not destroy my family life. How could I have known that life can be so cruel? That even though I was a young man of twenty-five, I was still no more than a child?

Wolf cracks a sad smile and so does Wiktor, gently exposing small, crooked teeth as he listens to Wolf's thoughts and looks out the window over his shoulder. Wolf's suit is made of fine wool that is uncommon in Poland, especially after the war. With his black, wavy hair, his dark clothes and beard, Wolf stands out from the crowd. A small group of militiamen, the law enforcement of Poland's communist regime, passes through the corridor of the train verifying passengers' identities. They stop to look at him.

"*Dokumenty*," the youngest of the threesome asks, a wry smile playing across his face.

Wolf removes from his pocket an American passport and hands it to the man. Wiktor notices how Wolf uses his left arm to hold the right one in place, doing what he can to conceal his trembling. The body exposes everything that the mind wishes to forget.

"What are you doing in Poland? Where are you going?" the young man asks in Polish, laughing derisively at the bald eagle on the cover of Wolf's passport. He opens the window in the train corridor and spits sunflower seed shells out the window as he speaks. Wolf's passport pages flutter in the wind as the young officer leans his elbow out the window, flailing his arm about. Pieces of shells leap between his teeth as he mocks the yid who has come back for a second beating.

Wolf takes a breath and sits up straight. Exhaling, he says, "I'm going to Białystok. To visit my family." His two fingers grab on to that little pink string on his pinky as if to say, *Nothing is going to happen to me baby, don't worry.*

"*You* have family there?" the militiaman asks, changing to Russian now.

Wolf replies in Russian.

"Yes, I do. I could not come to see them during the war, but now that the war is over, I am here. I am going back to America next week."

The militiaman takes a step back and one of his friends nudges him to move on.

"Okay, okay," he says, returning to Polish, handing Wolf back his passport, clinging to it for just a moment more.

The young man grasps the metal rack above Wolf's head and leans in so close that Wiktor has to move aside. His breath is labored and has the distinctly sweet smell of alcohol that has been lingering in the body all night long.

"Is it really like they say it is?" he asks Wolf. "You know, America. . . . Streets paved with gold. . . ."

Wolf sighs, knowing he has won. "It is that and so much more." *Much, much more.* The militiaman wrinkles the thick, smooth skin of his forehead and smiles quizzically, drunkenly, looking almost helpless, even innocent. He walks away without saying another word, and then moves on to train car number three, where a young schoolteacher is traveling alone with her sleeping child. He and his friends will wake her with their laughter, will pin her to the window while her child begins to cry, will lift her skirt and feel up her thighs, but they won't go any further, because just at that moment a stranger will walk into her car to ask for a light for his cigarette, and the militiamen will retreat, giddily. The woman will pull down her skirt, sweating and trembling her way into the early morning light. *Here I am, shaking again,* she will say to herself. *I couldn't stand up right now even if I wanted to. For how many more years will I have to shake and remember?*

Wolf looks out the window and exhales. Buds are blossoming along the road to the tune of a bittersweet cry. Those little birds, they sing with delight no matter what is happening on this earth. Their songs can shower this world with blessings, signaling the beauty of a new day, but they can also be the final arrow to remember how beautiful life once was and how it can never come back together again. To catch the shadows cast by the sun, to see the dawn coming, to live again.

Wolf closes his eyes. The sun is strong as it rises above the landscape, and Wolf stands momentarily to draw the curtain closed. As he blocks out the sun, he is reminded of how beautiful his sister looked that last summer, when they spent the day by a lake, swimming with friends and laughing. She was the only one who knew about Olga, but wouldn't dare let on what she knew. When Wolf's parents found out his secret, they were so upset that when they spoke about it they would shout with rage, so they just never spoke. He remembers his sister's blue eyes and her wide mouth that seemed to embrace the world with its laughter. He sits down again and closes his eyes. *Memories are beautiful, but they also keep pain alive. Would it be better to forget?*

Images of Rybnik, the German soldiers, of Elżbieta, and of his beloved wife, Waleria, standing at the kitchen table flash across Wiktor's mind in a whitewash of images while he watches Wolf struggle to find some peace. His wife's beautiful pale blue eyes always smiling, and her hands, fleshy and almost masculine in their strength and ability, always soothing his world-weary hands and feet. She knew how to make magic happen every evening when he came home from work.

Wiktor looks to the still dark western horizon, as yet untouched by the rising sun, and sees something that resembles a vision. It begins with a woman on a train. Not the same train they are on, but a similar one. Unlike the train to Białystok, this train carries the ones who have died but who have yet to pass on. They are like him, only different. This train moves so fast but rarely arrives anywhere. It just goes back and forth and back and forth. Dressed in housecleaning rags, a white cloth tied around her head, this woman sits in the empty train car staring out at the world. In her world it is darkest night, and snow lines the tracks that take her through the countryside. You can see all the Polish landmarks on her face: the sweeping planes of her cheekbones, the long blue eyes, the pronounced nose and the narrow lip. Gone is the happy glow of life.

Dark night. She is going west and they are going east. Her hands are folded in her lap. *I can wait for all eternity, but he will never come,* she says to herself. This is the mantra that passes the time. She still holds the ghosts of his mother, his father, his sister, in her pockets. She washed herself in their ashes before it was her turn to go, just so she could keep them with her, so that in this world and even in the next she could tell him that she had kept her word. *This love may transform, but it never dies,* she thinks. Soft fuzzy world, this country of hers, which shifts from brown to gray to periwinkle blue. She had always wished to travel to a place where there are palm trees, where oranges grow wild and the sun shines all winter long, but she never got farther than the Black Sea. In the distance tiny lights sparkle like Christmas tree ornaments as the green-gray light of the train car flickers. Christmas was always magical. She remembers it like yesterday. But nothing was ever so mesmerizing as the candlelit cemeteries on All Saints Day. She hums a tune to herself. Wiktor can hardly hear it, but he knows it is familiar. *A lullaby,* he thinks. She catches sight of the city lights approaching. Warsaw looks a little bit like the end of the world.

She turns to look back at Wiktor, or rather, Wiktor sees her looking at him, and when the train comes to a full stop he can see that she is completely gone. The half-light of dawn comes through the blinds to take her place. There is a silence as passengers descend from the train at Warsaw's main railway station, Warszawa Główna, a meeting place for all souls. Wiktor wonders just where the sad and beautiful lady went. Where is her train now, and when will he see her again?

XIII

We tried to get out once by ourselves, but it was no use. After a long struggle with crowbars and songs we were able to unlock the heavy school door, but when we walked out in a group, all forty-one of us, we found that we could go no further. The gate was locked in ways that even a man, ten meters high with hands made of steel, could not pry open, not even with all his might. These locks were made of inhuman strength, of heartache and endless regret. I cannot explain any better. My words have become different since the war and I can tell you things only the best way I know how. Words and letters are like waves moving in and out of my tongue. Sometimes they have no meaning, and at other times they seem to recreate the world.

I tried to get little Sarah, the youngest and smallest, to slide her body beneath the wrought iron gate so she could break the lock open from the other side. I had hoped she could help us get out. I even wished that this special job might give her a boost of confidence, encourage her to join the group a bit more. But when Sarah got close to the ground, she began to scream and could go no further. She refused to tell us what was on the other side. After about an hour of hysterics, she gave in and spoke.

"What we see from here, the town and the church and the smoke stacks from the factories, none of it was there when I peaked out from under the gate," she told us. "All I could see was dead bodies. Please don't make me try again. They won't let us out, that much I can tell. They were howling at me to go back in."

Then I asked Sarah, for she comes from a rabbinical lineage, and may also have some Gypsy roots, because she is afraid of nothing. She lay down on the floor and did not dare to scream as Sarah had, but simply stood up very quickly, dusted off her uniform skirt, and said that little Sarah was right, that there was no way we could get out that way. Then she looked at me sort of sideways and said, eyes wide, eyebrows knit together in an oddly mature way, "Besides, where exactly would we go?"

The girls all whispered as they marched back toward the looming schoolhouse, arm in arm. I took little Sarah by the hand and we walked slowly behind the rest of them, first stopping to look up at the new moon and the stars. That pale crescent moon was so delicate and tender that it made me remember the old days when I thought that the mere existence of such a tiny jewel in the night sky meant no harm could ever come to me or to the ones I loved. Now I look at the moon like a star-crossed lover. I look at you, and I believe in your majesty, but I am also afraid of what you can take away. I look at you, and I still want to believe. Believe that you can keep what is beautiful and make it real again. Believe that you can liberate us all, Sarah and Sarah and Sarah, and then that you can give us final freedom in that most beautiful unknown. If we are dwelling in that nothingness of the divine soul, then I believe it is you who will take us home.

I look down at little Sarah with her tear-stained cheeks and I want to hold her tight and never let go. I want to tell her all this and more, but it is too much for her young mind, even if it is enough for her ancient soul.

XIV

Warszawa Główna is indeed a meeting place for all souls. Wolf awakens to eat a sandwich wrapped in a brown paper bag. Wiktor notices that there is only cheese and lettuce in the sandwich, and he wonders how Wolf will have enough energy to get through the trip, but of course there is nothing much that he can say about it, and even if he were alive and could talk he still wouldn't ask. He doesn't know much about Jewish life, and he assumes that this delicate sandwich, which reminds him so much of the ones that his son, Karol, and his daughter, Elżbieta, used to eat when they were children, has something to do with the rules of this man's culture. Wiktor and his wife used to tease the children when they ate those sandwiches, calling them their little birds, but this man looks nothing like a delicate bird.

What do I know about their culture? Wiktor asks himself. *I know the dark eyes and skin that is sometimes, but not always, darker. I know they have two days reserved for God, and we have only one. People complain about this. They want to know what makes them so special? What else do I know? My wife's parents used to sell milk from their cows to the Jews, because the milk was known around the town for being the most pure, and Jews are always searching for cleanliness, or at least that's what I've been told. I never knew one until now.*

Spring is bursting along the tracks, but Wolf remembers the heavy snowfall that descended like a veil upon the world the day he and his new bride, Chaja, left the Old World. His mind wanders.

I remember my parents' hopeful faces and how their tears mingled with the snow. My father and I rarely embraced, but that day I took him into my arms. I felt as if I would die there on the spot. And I would have been happy to do so rather than to suffer the pain of leaving them behind. I was going into the unknown. The starched collar of my father's white shirt was drenched with tears, and I felt him tremble from somewhere deep inside. My mother took his hand in hers to keep him upright. Did they know somewhere inside that they would never see me again? I imagined that my parents were saplings that would recede into the earth for the winter, and when spring came, no matter where I lived in the world, they would just come back to life. But it wasn't true. Later I would discover just how deeply buried they were in my soul, that even death could not break us apart, for they echoed in my heart and in my genes. I see them in my children's faces. They are everywhere.

I remember that morning like it was yesterday. I went into the forest at dawn, walked through deep snow to find her there, waiting for me. Olga was standing in her pale gray sheepskin coat, blond curls surrounding her face in a halo, leaning against the trunk of my poplar tree. That was my tree, and she knew it. She had chosen that spot to make an impression on me, for she was nature and she was mine. Her eyes were red and puffy and I could see that she had been crying, but the expression on her face was one of complete resignation. It was cold, but her pale skin was warm. Here I was, following my parents' wishes to leave Poland. Four months earlier I had also agreed to marry my cousin Chaja.

Never in my life did I love Olga more than I did that morning when I knew I was leaving. Chaja was at my parents' house, sitting with our luggage, talking and drinking tea. She was laughing with my sister, who likely begged her to sing Yiddish songs, to dance and sing. That was the last moment of my life in Poland, and I was going into the forest toward my greatest desire. Did I know that it was my last chance to feel that pleasure? I felt so wild that nothing could have kept her from me. I would have ripped off my own skin if it would have brought us closer.

I remember that mad black crow as it flew overhead and I lifted her skirt and fell against her breasts. We remained standing as my black woolen coat spread open against the jagged bark of the tree, and I remained inside her. After four years of never giving in, we finally were able to feel each other from the inside out, and in that moment there was no greater perfection on this earth and maybe even in the heavens above. Her breath became mine, and when she quivered, it felt like an earthquake inside me, yet we hardly moved at all. For five years I had walked that forest and stared at that tree, but only now could I begin to understand what it felt like to be a man.

*

White birch trees lost in the passing snow. Count the twigs that line the road and crunch beneath the wheels as we go. I see those jagged white lines like frozen beings shattering the light. They pass so fast that they turn from many into one, casting time and space aside. They become more than a forest of trees, but a great wave swelling, gaining momentum and speed. I see their arms reaching out toward the sun. That light that is long forgotten on this earth. But the trees keep trying. They bury their roots in the snow and mud and wait for things to change. I remember how they witnessed our departure, and though they didn't show it, deep down in their innermost core, in the tiniest drop of sap that flows from unborn leaf in bud to ancient long-lived root, they wept for us. What else could they do with a living, breathing body frozen in time but stand there and wait for spring?

A tiny river is breaking through the icy ground and flowing from one end of the forest to another. Inconspicuous piles of snow melt and bleed into the water. Bare trees show their faces in reflective pools on the surface of the earth, birches hiding behind those majestic pines. The birch stands so bare, so naked, so beautiful because it cannot hide its vulnerability. Something is moving, something is alive in that dead, dead earth, and I remember how we passed that forest on our way to die. People suffocating like livestock in the hot train. Babies crying, and there was no milk, no water, not even air to feed our bleeding hearts. And how in the camp we sometimes ate the grass off the ground. It will take years for the birds to return now. For generations, there will be nothing for them to eat.

I washed my body with his mother's ashes so that I could tell him in the next life that we died together. So that I could make up for the fact that I was not born a Jew. Someday he will know that I loved him that much.

Life goes on. That water does still dare to flow. Sometimes, when I am not on this night train to Kraków, to Lublin, to Warsaw, or to the sea, I walk through the forests of my memory and I see Wolf and I making love against that poplar tree. I hear him breathing his soul into my ear and I remember what it was like to feel so alive. I remember his hands, surprisingly masculine, considering that all of his time was spent with books. I remember how they cupped my breasts, held my body so close to his that we could only become one. Two bodies and one breath heaving into the end of time.

I can walk through those forests and remember what it was like to smell the cold winter air or the spring, to breathe him in. Maybe those trees don't care who passes by anymore, or who lives or dies, but only that someone is living, that something is alive. Maybe they are real life, and we are just witnesses passing through dust. We make and live chaos, we are their enemy and we are their friend, and we are also that to each other. Sometimes on this train I recall the beauty of that life and I can feel what it was like to love and be loved. I remember what it was to *be*. Now I am caught between Białystok and Kraków, between life and death. On this train there are no other options but to exist in between.

XV

Mid-morning the train arrives in the eastern region of Podlasie. Leather bag in hand, Wolf disembarks the night train from Rybnik and walks across the platform at the Białystok train station. Wiktor follows him, free of all possessions. Footsteps sound hollow in the large, vacant room, and Wolf focuses his attention on the familiar walls, more decayed than ever, trying to maintain his composure. The men slowly cross the street and board a bus to the town of N.

A small dog with wiry hair, a fresh gash on his back, and big, dark eyes muddied by pale blue cataracts runs up to Wolf, begging to be touched. Wolf looks into the dog's moist eyes and pets the back of his neck gently. Whenever he dares to stop, the dog nudges him for more.

Even though the day is cool, the atmosphere on the bus is stuffy. Wolf sits near the window, and Wiktor is on the empty seat beside him. The small stray dog follows Wolf and curls himself into a ball at his feet. His eyes seek out the warm solace that lies in the fold of a pant leg, the carefully tied lace of a shoe, the comfort of a master.

Wolf pulls from his pocket three small gray stones, and in the secret hollow of his palm, he calls them by name. Backward, forward, the words still carry the same meaning: *mother, father, sister, siostra.*

These are the sounds that choke as Wolf thinks quietly to himself. *I can live my day, just breathing, just thinking, and then a sound catches in my throat and it becomes impossible not to cry.* But he doesn't cry in public anymore.

Within the hour they arrive in the town of N. Wiktor follows Wolf as he approaches the town bakery. Wolf stands staring. The building that once belonged to his wife, Chaja, and to her father before that, which was given to his mother when they left for America, has now been completely transformed. What was once the Chaim Sara Bakery, and which later became Chaja's Bread, is now called Mrs. Stania's Piekarnia. The same pine benches line the walls that were there before. The tall stools with seats covered in fine velvet that was used to upholster Chaja's family's home, which was leftover from the living room couch and sewn into cushions by his sister, Leye, still exist in that room. The same glass cases. . . .

"Okay let's move on," he mumbles to the dog, and the dog seems to listen.

On the street passersby take note of the man with dark hair dressed in a black suit made of lightweight summer wool, so much finer than their threadbare clothes. They take note of him, the stranger, who is detectable immediately as an outsider, but who is also as familiar as any other resident of the town.

The face that has come back to haunt them.

Wolf stops walking and sits on the steps of the old town hall in the market square, twirling those three little stones in his left hand. The town church bells ring, striking eleven, God's hour. Families dressed in their Sunday best walk toward the town church, while others head toward the Orthodox church on the other side of town. They glance over at Wolf as they run. *Why is he drawing attention to himself? What does he want from us? Why does he have to remind us when all we want is to forget the past?*

Wolf recognizes Pan Chełmiński, the town cobbler, by the peak of his old green hat. His sons, Jan and Paweł, who were kids when Wolf left home, but who now tower over their short, stocky father, are in tow. Jan and Paweł are twins who were in the same class as Wolf's little sister, Leye. Before the war, they would all go sledding together in the tiny hills just beyond the forest. Paweł even took Leye out on a date once, but their father never let her go farther than the movies. Paweł smiles at Wolf curiously, for he is surprised to see him. He lifts his hand to wave hello, and Jan knocks it down. The young men enter church behind two old ladies and a young family with several little girls. *None of these children with blond braids and starched dresses ever even knew a world before the war,* Wolf tells himself. *They are blessed in this life,* he thinks, standing, the little dog jumping at his feet. *They have nothing to remember, nothing to miss.* Wolf continues walking. There is no point in dwelling on a golden braid, a green hat, on the memory of what no longer is.

Down the street where boys used to sing in the rain, where Shabbat was spent strolling through town with his father, where he memorized a parsha for his bar mitzvah while walking in the forest until his feet were red with blisters. Down the street where he first saw a beautiful woman naked and dreamt of one day loving someone. Funny enough, it was Olga's aunt whom he first saw in the nude. She lived in the house beside Olga's, and would leave the curtains of her bedroom window open so that all the local boys could witness her perfectly naked form as she undressed every evening. She secretly knew that they were watching her, and it would be a lie to say that it did not give her some pleasure knowing that she was the object of their adoration. Her greatest dream was to be loved by everyone and become a great actress in Berlin.

Down the street where he would jump his neighbors' fence in order to quickly arrive at the back door. On Friday afternoons he would smell his mother's cooking from a block away, and with his mouth watering uncontrollably he would inevitably run through the neighbor's garden, taking the fastest route home. Flying with his jacket buttons undone, his kippah sliding from his head, all he wanted was to catch her with flour on her hands, baking challah or stirring soup. He would change his clothes and then the world would come to a halt. The candles would be lit and the songs sung.

Down this street there is nothing anymore. The little stray dog yelps as Wolf comes to a stop before the house that was once his home. Wiktor motions to the dog to be quiet, and, oddly enough, the dog listens.

Leye, Wolf begins, quietly and to himself, *if I could reach you now I would tell you this: the house where we once lived isn't empty anymore. A new family has moved in, and they are breaking bread for Sunday dinner. They are much taller and stronger than we were, but they seem so sad, as if the weight of the world is on their shoulders. They are solemn during their meal, passing dishes back and forth, sharing small talk, mostly about the weather. Remember how you would rise from the table and dance, and sometimes Mama would join you after Birkat Hamazon? Remember the colors of those silly Yiddish songs, and how you would wrap your long black braid like a rope around your head and pretend to be an old man with a beard? Remember the laughter and the jokes? Leyeleh, there is a family sitting down to dinner at our table now, and even though their dishes aren't ours, and their silverware is their own, I feel goose bumps rising on my back as I see them eating soup with our old silver spoons, see them drinking from Papa's cup. I cannot see things as they are. I want to look through the window and see you perched there on the arm of Papa's chair, reading with him, turning the pages, twirling your curls, adjusting the old lamp with the yellow stained-glass shade so that everything is just right, so that words can be illuminated and come to life.*

Wolf places the three smooth gray stones on the windowsill of his old home. The modesty of the stones has nothing to do with their meaning. He stands in the window in plain view, but nobody notices him from inside. He turns away from the image of strangers inhabiting his family home and walks toward the forest outside of town.

XVI

The cathedral where Saint Thérèse of Lisieux would pray as a child was so cavernous that even in summertime she wore a coat to protect herself from the cold. Pigeons dwelling in the rafters would fly overhead while she prayed, and during mass as she knelt before the altar she would listen to the rush of those humble gray wings, yearning for a time when she might be relieved of her painful sensitivity and feel at home in the world. As a child she suffered from nervous tremors and total despair. She felt happy and safe only when at home with her father and her sisters, but one Christmas she felt Christ fill her heart, and her life began anew. She was granted permission to enter the order of the Carmelite nuns at the age of fifteen, where she wrote her autobiographical texts, which would later become *l'Histoire d'une Âme* (*The Story of a Soul*). She once wrote, "The only way I can prove my love is by scattering flowers, and these flowers are every little sacrifice, every glance and word."

She died of tuberculosis when she was only twenty-four. Her last words were spoken to God, with love.

We have an illustrated book about Saint Thérèse here at the school library, which little Sarah loves best. Sarah usually tires easily, but she can sit for hours staring at the colorful drawings that depict Thérèse's childhood experiences and how she overcame her fears. She even reads long passages out loud to herself. Once I asked her just what it was about the Catholic saint that captured her attention, especially since she never even saw the inside of a church in her life, but she just looked at me wistfully with those long blue eyes and shrugged her shoulders carelessly.

"Don't know," she said, twirling a ringlet of her curly brown hair and staring up at the ceiling the way she does when she doesn't want to look somebody in the eye. "When I look at her," she added, "I feel happy."

"Fair enough," I told her, and put a red ribbon in her hair.

XVII

On bended knees Elżbieta twirls the delicate ring with a woven lattice pattern and a pale orange stone around the middle finger of her left hand. It doesn't fit her ring finger now, but someday it will. When she grows older and her fingers swell, the ring will fit her like a glove.

Her mother handed it to her yesterday when they came in from hanging laundry on the balcony. The ring was a gift from Wiktor after the depression, when Waleria had suffered a breakdown and spent several weeks in a sanitarium. The ring was a symbol of new beginnings.

They tried to hum a tune they used to sing before the war, but Elżbieta couldn't remember the words. It made her happy to see her mother singing, but at the sight of one of Wiktor's white collared shirts, the song soon came to an end. Waleria sat on the concrete floor of the balcony and cried into the folds of his wet shirt. Where once upon a time she would run into the kitchen and throw her apron on at the first signs of Wiktor's figure coming around the bend, now there was nowhere to go in anticipation of love. To the baby's basket, to the smell of his head and neck, and to the soft curl of his fingers and his lips. To the baby for comfort that there was still a future to come.

Elżbieta holds the ring in the late afternoon light and watches how it gleams pale orange. Things, beautiful things especially, are rare nowadays. To have something beautiful is a blessing. That thing, whatever it is, should be cared for with love and appreciation.

Elżbieta pulls from her pocket the faded photograph that she carries of St. Thérèse of Lisieux. She has been her patron saint ever since her first communion, and she takes their bond seriously, first by wearing a small pendant with Thérèse's likeness around her neck, and second, by praying to her every day. She whispers to her sweet little newborn that St. Thérèse will always take care of him. "Shhh," she says, "Do not worry, little Mateusz. When you are alone and afraid you can always pray to her and she will send down a shower of roses." She tucks the photo back into her dress pocket and crosses herself. She puts the ring back inside an ornate wooden box that she hides in a drawer beside her favorite sweater. She doesn't want her sisters to know that their mother gave it to her. She doesn't want anyone to know that she is the most beloved. It is a secret between her, her mother, and God.

XVIII

Never in his childhood will little Mateusz cast a stone. Not even when he is six and discovers the large pile of worms sewing newly turned earth in his father's vegetable garden. Not at the head of the dead sparrow that appears in his garden, so still and hidden, with pale yellow wings and a furry brown tendril passing from head to toe. Not when he discovers that bird on a warm, sunny day, when it seems that the whole world is smiling with the coming of spring. He will walk through the garden dancing, pointing out in his mind's eye each little chamomile flower as it pokes out from the grass, and then stumble across the tiny bird, still perfect, still whole, its beak sticking into the overgrown grass. There is a shudder that passes through his body at the sight of this perfect little creature still so alive in body but devoid of life. How can that be? Its head facing down, as if to teach Mateusz that there is always a price to be paid for new life. Like when Wiktor died around the time of his birth and during the coming of spring. *Why*, he will ask himself, now and forever after, *why does spring always bring death?*

Never a stone is thrown. Not even just to see if that little bird can move again.

And when Mateusz will turn eight years old and return home from a weeklong trip to the sea with his grandmother, Waleria, to heal his stomachaches that come every other day or so, he will gather his newfound strength and learn archery. Never a stone has been thrown, but one day he will go out into the forest with his friends from down the road, his little brothers tagging along, the middle brother sitting on the handlebars of his bicycle, and the youngest on his shoulders while he rides. He is so talented with a bow and arrow that he wants to show off to his little brother and his friends his tight white shorts and the long lean muscles on his legs. He chooses a target on an old pine tree, but when Wojtek, his classmate, jumps before the pine, Mateusz misses piercing his face by a fraction of a second. Both boys run home crying, and neither one of them ever picks up a bow and arrow again. In fact, these two boys will cease to be friends. They still run around in the same little pack, but it will be years before they talk or look into each other's eyes again. Wojtek remains afraid of Mateusz, and Mateusz, when he looks into Wojtek's eyes, can see only his own vulnerability, and there is nothing so frightening in this world.

XIX

In the forests of Podlasie, spring is the reward for an endless snowfall and for the mud that follows. Wolf walks slowly away from the market square in the southern part of town, passing the old mikveh on Ulica Szkolna. Besides this charred and empty space is blackened ground that was once occupied by the central synagogue. Down the street in the house where the rabbi once lived there is now a storage room for the town. Abandoned chairs and desks and unused doors can be seen through the broken, stained glass windows. Stuffed velvet couches, ornate mirrors, mezuzahs scattered on the floor.

Wolf closes his eyes in order to see what was. He sees the rabbi at the bimah, and his father standing with him, opening the gates to the Torah. He recalls his own bar mitzvah, reciting his parsha, and the excitement of remembering, of being honored, of becoming a man.

Wolf continues to walk toward the forest with Wiktor and the little stray dog in tow. It is Sunday, yes, and the town seems empty as people find themselves hidden at home or in church. Not one store is open, not one public space has movement, none other than the town square where people are sitting outside after church, or the train station where people come and go.

Leather bag slung over his shoulder, Wolf takes careful footsteps as branches crunch beneath his feet. He makes his way to a desolate graveyard, a large pile of stones in its center.

*

When gravestones crumble they look just like any other ruin. A pile of rock in a desert or a field, a forest hidden from those who wish to forget. It begins with a word. A word marks the beginning, the destruction, that which binds me to you. If you reverse the letters you may find the hero inside. This is the last word. These tombstones are scattered letters, sparks of light, the Torah destroyed, Shekinah's whisper in the night.

How can you identify which stones belonged to him? And which to her? They are all jumbled together. Some still stand, but they are only half of what once was. They have become a massive pile of rock, a jigsaw puzzle that might never be solved. I know. I have stood at the base of that pile and tried to envision their reconstruction, but I tell you, there is no way. They are the Pyramid of Giza, the pantheon opening up its vast eye to the gods. They are a testament to a people forgotten.

A call to the forgotten ones. Will you hear their sound? Look on them, the fragments of graves, and none of them say your family name. None of them tells the brief story of your mother, Sara Ain, beloved wife of Menachem, mother to Leye and Wolf, 1902–1942. None but you. You tell it. And even though you feel as if you are in the dark, there is a world spinning around you, and all those souls are waiting to hear their name called. Tell it.

*

There are certain words that cannot reach Wolf's lips without getting caught in a net of despair. Words get locked where they should be expelled. They hover in the air that lingers between breaths, returning to his body where they reside in the chest as woeful and unrelenting pain. There are some words that, once spoken, hit the brain like a signal that brings the truth to mind, words you have to live and go on living. You have to bring new life into this world and not fear for it this destiny. You must tell this life about the beauty and joy of living and try to forget. But in your deepest whisper that flows from your veins down to your child's, you will say, *Inside these immoveable walls there is a story to tell,* and you will know it without knowing it, and it will be the secret that is spoken through actions and not words. It will be alive in your genes, and in your life you will speak it silently, but it will show in your movement and in your deepest fears. There are certain words that cannot be sung, even though they are this song. They catch in the throat and return to your heart, from which nothing must escape, and so you breathe slowly, carefully, never to breathe in her love again.

Wolf stands amid a sea of matzevot, a pile of rubble that was once the Jewish cemetery of N, and begins to recite the Kaddish, the prayer for the dead. He knows there should be nine other men standing with him, but it doesn't matter today. Those nine men are lost in the ashes of a forgotten world. They are scattered in Bełżec, Auschwitz, Birkenau, Treblinka, in the forests near Zabłotczyzna, names that will occupy his mind for a lifetime. He sings for them, for his mother and father, for his sister, Leye, and for Olga, who burns bright inside him. She died trying to save them. Who will save her now?

*

Wolf, if only you could see me now. "Olga," you would whisper, saying my name the way no one else can, but I know you would be afraid. My face is so pale, I cannot recognize my own reflection. How I missed you during the war, but how grateful I was that you were not there to see me anymore. How I thanked the heavens that you could not witness the anguish and fear that ravaged my face and body, leaving me a remnant of myself. I clung to the image of myself in your mind. I remembered that girl, too, that beautiful me.

In the distance, the lights of Kraków look like fairytale lanterns decorating the pages of a storybook life. They remind me of a story I used to read as a child before I went to sleep at night. It was about a Swedish family that celebrated Santa Lucia every year at Christmastime. They knew well how to illuminate the night. I see those lights and how they want to sparkle bright, keep hidden the stories that passed through those Wisła River waters in recent years. Who is it who wants to tell of how the world was divided into parts; of how if you could not adhere to this division you would lose your life; and even if you did adhere, you might lose your life anyway? Those parts still remain. That separation will stay. This game of lottery took from you first what you loved, and then your beloved. Who wants to tell the story of how the Jews were taken first from their homes and led into a ghetto, and then pulled and pulled, heart at its seams, those walls that separated the world of color from a realm of gray despair? And who chose which world on the inside? Don't ask me again why I chose to abandon my freedom. For me, love was always more important.

Oh Wolf, how this train does hoot and howl as it pulls into the Kraków station. Not the station you know of, not the one that takes you into town, but the one that took us away. To where the track ends, leading nowhere. This is where my train comes in, where the duchy, the spirits, get on and off. Those little fairy lights can only distract for so long. If only I could go into the Jewish cemetery and bury myself in the earth, praying that it accepts me at last. May some great force of life take pity on me and let me be free.

*

This prayer offers freedom from pain for the one still living: Even though I walk.

Even though I walk, I shall not want.

In this prayer there is a valley and a shadow and someone to guide.

People need to believe that there is always someone there to comfort, even on the other side.

Sometimes Sarah and I like to imagine which movie star we would marry if we could. We found a silent movie magazine on an old dusty bookshelf in the library, and when we are happy and gay we all agree that it is the most fascinating thing in the world. All of us but little Sarah, who sits above us perched on top of the stuffed velvet chair at the corner of the room reading St. Thérèse of Lisieux's book *l'Histoire d'une Âme*. She is stubborn and curious, and I love her all the more for it. If only I could soothe her heart just a little more, then mine would feel lighter as well. But I am bound just like everyone else to the uniform, to the dress. I am bound to be, I am bound to love, I am bound to Sarah.

*

The Wisła River may be of comfort to some, but not me. Would drown myself in her waters and die a second death if I could. I see her as a silent truth teller, a witch's brew leaking the fires of Smok, Wawel Castle's dragon, down through Kraków's riverbanks, swollen and pregnant with pain and regret. Behind this sixteenth-century hand-carved icon of Madonna and Child lies a secret you'll know one day. How many Jews converted in this very chapel? I'll tell you: many. Behind this door, a relic of dreams left behind. This doorstep. This candle. This whisper, this vestment hangs in perfect order. Some say we Poles were ordered by God to serve as martyrs for all humankind. "The Christ of all nations," our beloved romantic poet, Mickiewicz, once called us, but I say, let's spare ourselves that title once and for all.

There are no forests in Kraków to remind me of you. No birch trees to stand naked and witness what passes them by, so I close myself to the world and hold that image of us entwined against a tree in my mind as I walk. Here there are only cobblestones lining the streets. They amplify the cacophony of horse and carriage, of human footfall as it passes, even of butterfly wings as they brush the ground, but I can assure you that my feet don't make a sound.

*

A thick blanket of moss covers the ground beneath Wolf's feet. The prayer for the dead moves inward, the words, the letters retreating down his throat. Drops form a puddle at his feet as a stream pours from his face into the earth. He has the thought that he is participating in creation. This water will help the flowers and grass to grow, and they will crowd the pile of rubble, ultimately covering it. Nature will bury the buried and swallow the lost. *Why would I wish to contribute any life to this place that has taken so much life from me? Why would I smile at the sight of one petal blooming on account of my tears?* Wolf drops his prayer book and lifts his hands to cover his face, wanting to stop the water from flowing and hide himself from the world.

Wiktor steps a few meters away from Wolf. They cut two lonely figures in this forest where all of the local peoples have mixed at one point or another: Russians, Poles, and also Jews. Slight Wiktor with his dark skin, cropped hair, and loose pants stands with his once clean, now invisible worker's hands thrust into his pockets watching Wolf as he tries to stop his own tears.

Or maybe the salt from my tears will kill all life within reach? Perhaps my pain will be transmitted into the earth, and caterpillar skulls will soon line the route taken by ants and spiders, and everyone who passes will know that death lived here.

Wiktor looks around at this forest in the prime of spring. The ground is still wet with mud, but in the air trees transition from bud to blossom in an instant. Tiny white puffs of pollen are carried on the wind, transported from tree to tree, from flower to flower, and eventually down to earth. Wiktor wishes he could breathe once again and smell the sweet dampness of springtime. Now he knows there is no stopping this world from continuing without the ones we love, and even without ourselves that we have also loved. This is our bittersweet destiny, to love and build a world, a house, a body of our own, and then to discard it all.

*

Wolf stands to retreat from the pile of stones. Tears, like words, move back down the throat and into the heart. There is such a thing as an ache in the heart. The breeze picks up and a flood of pollen floats through the air. *If my daughter were here, I would tell her that this is a kingdom of fairies coming to greet her. What will I tell myself? Is this a sign that they hear me now? And now?* And for just a moment, Wolf can almost detect their whisper in the wind.

Wolf knows that it is time to go. He wipes his face, turns away from the rubble and from the remaining stones, gathers his book and his bag, and whistles for the little dog to come. The dog comes running eagerly, a clump of old leaves stuck to his back.

It is time for Wolf to leave town. But leaving town is not as easy as it might seem. First, there is the pull of memories and the knowledge that after today he will likely never see this place again. It is so tempting to walk back through the streets, to stand at the corner that looks out over the remnants of synagogues and homes, to find something to remember them by.

A rose from my mother's garden. I could wrap the stem in wet paper and try to keep it alive until I get back to America. I could replant it in the backyard in Brooklyn. And the rose bush would blossom every spring. . . .

Church services are letting out and people are strolling through town, ice cream cones in hand. Young and old, every Pole loves ice cream to assure them that summer has arrived at last. The townspeople have not yet made it over to the back streets, where Wolf is already walking, Wiktor and the dog in tow.

Wolf considers going back the way he came, but instead decides to take a different route, one that will get him in and out of town more quickly. He passes a row of old houses on Ulica Nadrzeczna, all of them completely quiet, their lights dim, except for one. From an open window, the sound of a somber piano can be heard. Chopin études mix with the smell of boiling potatoes and the aroma of freshly chopped parsley and dill filling the air along with the sounds of romantic heartbreak, and for a moment, Wolf can close his eyes and recall another life: Mama standing in the kitchen, dinner waiting on the table, Leye sitting at the piano, Papa at his desk, an open book before him, his mind traversing the world. The only thing separating Wolf from his past is a closed eyelid. A closed eyelid has the capacity to usher in another world.

Cloud cover is drifting into town, and though the sun is still visible on the horizon, a cool breeze stirs the air, lifting dried leaves and shuttling them across empty streets. The sweet damp smell of rain penetrates the air, and Wolf pulls his collar up around his neck to shield his throat from the wind. *If it isn't really cold, then why do I feel so chilled?* A black crow flies overhead as a shiver runs up the small of Wolf's back. Wiktor stands behind Wolf, scanning the misty landscape.

They now come to the dim alleyway that leads the group back to number eleven Ulica Nadrzeczna, the location of Wolf's childhood home. Equidistant from the forest and the market square, this house was the perfect place to grow up, but it was also one of the first homes to be searched for liquidation when the Nazis arrived.

"How lucky we are," Wolf's parents told one another from their quiet hovel in the attic apartment provided by Wolf's friend, Olga. What good fortune they had that Olga was such a kind woman. Jew or no Jew, she knew what was coming before it came and was willing to risk her life for them. Hiding a Jew meant your entire family (and sometimes even your neighbors) could be killed, and yet many Poles did it anyway.

Every afternoon Olga would climb the stairs and bring them bread and cheese, a bottle of boiled water, and sometimes even a jug of cold coffee. She would also carry a bucket of water for them to wash in, and then to use as a toilet. She would then deposit the bucket in the outhouse while her mother was at church. At the start of the war Olga's father was sent to a camp in Siberia, but because of the family's prominent standing in the town, Olga and her mother were lucky enough to remain at home. Her mother believed that prayer would keep her husband safe. She would not discover, until six months after the war, that her husband had died in transport on the way to the Soviet Union. Before hard labor and devastation could destroy him, he was taken by dehydration and starvation. "Better to die that way," she would say as she cried herself to sleep. "My beloved," she would whisper into her husband's pillow, "better that you did not have to destroy those beautiful strong hands in the cold harsh winter of that labor camp. It may be better, but I will never be the same." By the time she received news of her husband's death, her house was empty and she was alone. The war took from her everything she loved, and she would whisper to the photographs on the wall, the lace trim on the cuffs of her blouse, the candles lit on the pyre, "See what life stole from me in the night?"

"How lucky we are," Wolf's parents would whisper to one another when the silence was booming. Young Leye had begun to experience moments in which she felt that she could not breathe, times when a ringing in her ear would become deafeningly loud, and she would then hold her head beneath the pillow, trying to drown out the sound. The walls and the world were closing in on her. Maybe she knew more than her parents that there really was no chance of escape. Maybe having lived less made her believe less in the world.

"Just think, my little darlings," her father would say, in his most delicate and caring voice, "just think how lucky we are that we will survive this terrible time. Wait and see, things will be set right in this world."

Were there smiles that also broke through the clouds and cobwebs of their faces on those dark attic days? Yes, of course there were. There were howls of laughter emitted during the church-going candlelit hours, and there were yelps let loose into the lumpy old down pillow when silence was a necessity and tiny white feathers poked out through invisible holes, getting caught in Leye's long black hair. Were there tears that formed puddles on the floor? Small pools of water with nowhere to go that you swept into the deep grooves of old planks of cherry wood? Were those tears absorbed by the grains of wood? Were they absorbed and later reborn, coming to life as pale moth's wings? And how did you feel at the sight of Papa, always strong and wise, the backbone of our life, as he cried just like the rest of us, destroying your image of a solid and perfect world?

"How lucky we are, my darling," Wolf's father would say to his wife as he stroked her face and hair. But luck was not on their side. Olga's family home was just steps away from the market square. Her house could not be overlooked for long.

Yes, they were lucky, Wolf tells himself, looking up at incoming clouds. *At least they died in each other's arms.*

Wolf wonders if the only happy time in your life is when you are a child. Your mother holds you in her arms, gives you milk and bread, and bathes you as tenderly as if you were still in her womb. You are no more than caterpillar legs, a sun-kissed heart, and still your hand is always held tight.

As if it were yesterday. As if it were yesterday that we were sitting together in this garden beneath the gentle sky. Mother made apple cake and compote, and we sat in the shade of the big cherry blossom tree laughing and talking as if we had all the time in the world. Night would come, and we continued to sit, enjoying each other's company in the dark.

The stray dog with dark eyes gives out a small sigh and rustles through a trash can, pulling a pile of vegetable peels across the ground, dragging them along the gnarled roots of the old cherry blossom tree. Wiktor stands beside the rose bush as Wolf reaches to break off a stem, his eyes closed, as if he is remembering the most beautiful and quiet dream. There is a faint whisper, a shout, and then a door swings open. Wiktor turns to look back at the house, and just as the door opens, a stone flies through the air.

There is a thump like a knock on the brain, and then nothing.

Beneath the cherry blossom tree lies a crumpled rose.

There are so many ways to encounter blood. There is the blood that comes from pricking one's finger with thorns, the blood you tasted when you were a curious child and you wanted to know. You needed to understand intimately the taste of tears, the taste of blood, how people make love, why the clouds look that way, and is God there, and what (on a coldest darkest night, you would ask) happens when we die? Where do we go? Is it just black and then nothing? Nothing? Nothing? How can there be nothing?

What exists in this nothingness? Is it black and is it silent? Do wild flames encircle bodies tortured by impure thoughts? Does a white light beckon you forward? Are you freed from the earth's shackles, and like Dante at last encountering his Beatrice, do you rise up and go into the petals of that brilliant white celestial rose? Do you want to go? Do you let go? For Wolf there are no white lights. He is the last spark of light in this lonely place. There is no mirror to reflect his beauty back to him anymore.

Wolf awakens to water rushing onto his face. Rain is pouring down and the ground is wet, mud rising like a tidal wave around him, as if nature were protesting his defeat. Struck by nauseating pain and by an unbearable ringing in his ears, Wolf instinctively touches his face.

There is red and there is shouting.

"You'd better go fast, *żydku* (little Jew), otherwise you'll join your family in that forest sooner than you think."

These are words taken from the atmosphere, from the world, from the mind of a man on the run. Wolf stumbles toward the train station, a stream of blood dripping down his face and through his fingers, bag hanging loosely from his shoulder. His limbs feel disjointed, his heart races and his mind screams, *You won't get me. Never!*

The train leaves the station.

Wiktor holds Wolf's aching head tenderly in his arms.

*

In the dream he comes for me at night. Sarah and I spend the day building a small wooden house for little Sarah's toys, and we lose track of time as the sun grows huge, settling in the west. The room is aglow. We feel as if we are sitting in the belly of the sun.

Sarah throws back her long, shining black hair, and she stares at me with those slanted blue-gray eyes. "Let's walk up to the roof," she says, smiling wickedly, raising her left eyebrow the way she always does whenever she has an idea. I find it impossible to say no. The day is warm enough to shed our sweaters, and we sit on the hot tin roof overlooking the factories of Łódź. I always enjoyed the rolling hills of the Polish countryside, but this is our landscape now. Sarah can name more than half of the companies and point out what each factory produces and what kind of machinery it uses. Before the war her father owned the biggest factory in town, and she used to spend school holidays helping his secretary to address letters in his office, which is why she had such perfect penmanship at a young age and also how she learned to walk in high heels.

Before the war, Łódź was a town of three languages and three cultures. There were Germans, Jews, and Poles. I wonder what it is like now with no Jews and no Germans? No one to be punished or do the punishing? Factories with no owner and no name? Sarah and I sit and imagine together how things might have changed in Łódź with no more Jews observing Shabbat. Together we light candles every Friday at sundown, with no challah, only ourselves. Sometimes we forget all of the words to the prayers and just have to hum the tune, but we know that this is okay. Our parents, wherever they are, would be proud of us. When we sing, at least one of us is bound to be sad and long for the past. Little Sarah used to get so moody that she wouldn't even join our Shabbat celebrations, but things have changed and now she even asks to light the candles. The rest of us decided to give her the job, because even though we know that she will never grow older, we agree that it is important to give her the chance to feel more grown up. The truth is that none of us knows when Friday has come, nor do we know what will come in the future, but we do our best to count sunrises and sunsets and to keep a schedule. We observe Shabbat as best we can. Every seven days we stop what we are doing, and that is the best we can do.

In the dream Sarah and I have a wonderful time talking and laughing on the roof. This is not so different from our regular life. She does cartwheels across the still-hot tin as the moon takes center stage before our eyes. We return to our rooms and hang our uniforms side by side, lying down to rest on a row of cots. All these Sarahs with their uniforms hanging above.

I cannot sleep. I toss and turn and sit up in bed to watch the full moon from my window. I talk to the moon, as I always have, both in real life and in the afterlife. I smile and sense the moon smiling back. It speaks to me without movement or sound, and I hear all that it says. It calls me Rachelka. It speaks to me by name. Birth name, given name, name chosen by my mother, by my father, name called out by my little brother, my real name, Rachelka.

"Tonight is the night you get set free," it says to me in that liquid silver whisper that makes no audible sound. Tonight I know nothing about Sarah. I smile and fall briefly into sleep, where I enter a dream within a dream.

From my bed I sense that someone is at the gate. I rise and go down to greet whoever it is, noticing that I am not even wearing my nightgown. My body is wrapped in a shimmering sheet, a sheet that blows in the wind and feels both rough and cool against my skin as I walk down the cold stone staircase. Stepping out into the schoolyard, I am illuminated by the pale moonlight. I am sheathed in the desert wind and in this moment I feel as if I am the moon, the stars, the desert, the night. I am nature and, for the first time, I am also a woman.

A man stands at the gate waiting for me. He has blue eyes that twinkle in the light and wavy gray hair. He also has many wrinkles on his face, but he still looks young and handsome. He smiles at me as if he knows about me, why I am here and why I am leaving. He unlocks the gate, just like that, and then he remains at his post, as if his presence will protect me no matter where I go. I step out into the city street and enjoy the movement of the golden sheet as it flaps in the moonlit wind, brushing against my body. After so much time spent inside the school, the city has changed. I can see that many years have passed. There are more cars on the street than ever before, and there are young men with shaved heads standing around a fire wearing sport clothes, drinking from big bottles, laughing, breaking their bottles into the fire and watching with glee as they shatter. There are women laughing and talking, drinking along with them. They wear short skirts and bright blue makeup on their eyes. They look just like the women who used to hang out by the train station at night when I was a child.

My city has transformed into a lost and forgotten ghost town. I wander the streets looking at the people and the empty houses. Nobody can see me now. The overwhelming grayness has swallowed up many of the once beautiful buildings, and though I feel sorry for what has happened, I cannot say that I feel much regret. In the dream I am one with the night, and nothing can take from me my ecstasy.

*

The feather and I are coming closer and closer to each other, and whenever the sun rotates 'round us I wonder if this time will be the last. What life will we be born into next, and how painful will it be to leave this suspended existence? Just how will we know when it is time to say goodbye?

Part II
Anna and the Child

I

It is easy to swallow the magic pill, for it is small and can be ingested with ease. That's right, this pill grows on trees. In pools of muddy water covered with dried, forgotten leaves you can also find this pill and you can take it and all things will be healed. In this place you can find it everywhere, and it is available to everyone for free. When you are in trouble, you can remember this. When you are ill or sad you can close your eyes and ask for this pill and then you can find it out in the woods or even where there is no more green to be seen. Even on cobblestone streets, in concrete, it will be there waiting for you. When you take it, you can jump like a grasshopper. You can remember everything that you want to remember and nothing that you want to forget. This pill makes life beautiful and erases all pain.

Ever since I discovered this pill, I take one every day. I walk through the woods outside of town and I pick one, for they grow wild, like mushrooms. Wild. You may think that if one is good then more than one could be even better, but one is enough to change your world. I am telling you about this because I know what you're feeling. I can see that you experienced what I experienced, and who knows, some things may be worse. But I can tell you that there is a way out. And it has nothing to do with the Red Cross or Joint

Distribution Committee or the church. You can go to Ulica Długa 38 to check the slips of paper, the wall of names, to see if your family has returned, but it won't help. You won't find their names anywhere but in the dust. This pill will make you forget your family, and then you will feel no pain.

I first discovered it when I was transported to a camp near Kraków. I was with my father, but then we were separated, and an old man took me under his wing and told me about the pill that would help me to survive. He was right. I made it here because of this pill I will show you now, the one that will help change your life.

II

His hand is small and delicate, like that of a young pianist, or of one who has not yet withstood the test of time. The nails on his fingers are jagged and deep grooves of dirt form beneath them. His face is constructed of wide smooth planes, and just like a baby's, his skin shows no indication of worry, no scars to suggest the things he has seen. His eyes are a glassy blue, long in the way many of his countrymen's eyes are long. They recall the Mongol. They are a reminder that racial purity does not exist. Not even in Poland.

The boys emerge from a small cluster of trees that cast shade across an old brick wall stretching from one block to the next. Staggered but together, they make their way back into the street. The older boy, the leader of the two, walks in front of the little one, who is no more than seven years old but who has the look of a wrinkled old man who has seen enough and wants to close his eyes to the world. The leader is adolescent but small, his oversize shirt, stolen off a corpse one year ago, rolled up at the sleeves. Here is Ulica Szewska, one of many passageways leading to the market square. Streets stretch out from the center of Kraków like the many arms of Ganesh reaching past the obstacles of the world. If only they could. Leaving the market square they pass the cool shade of Planty, a ring of green surrounding the city center. In winter, Planty is a wonderland in miniature—branches bending down to cover pedestrians from the snow, though the walkway is covered with ice and it is inevitable that someone will fall. Ah, but in summertime the very same place is imbued with the sweet smell of lilac, and people walk slowly. They sit and talk, enjoy an ice cream cone. Grown men in their short-sleeve shirts with starched collars sit and lick to their heart's content. Suddenly everyone becomes a child. Here the boys make their way slowly, oversize shoes toiling against the uneven cobblestones.

Anna is heading toward Planty while they are walking in the direction of the market square. Maybe today they can find a little work, or else some food to eat behind one of the few still-operating cafés.

When you want to walk like a lady you arch your back, extend your buttocks, relax your face. When you do it well, nobody notices the pain with which you step or the black seam drawn up the backside of your leg. She is focused on the pain in her feet, the rumbling in her stomach, but it is the feeling of fear that causes her to lift her gaze and notice the boys, as if fear is a forward-cast shadow preceding the one whom it is devouring, alerting the public to its presence. The first boy is no more than eleven or twelve years old. He passes by, eyes holding her gaze long enough to make her recognize his suffering. She feels his hunger, and it makes her shudder someplace deep within. She looks away quickly. As if he could take something away from her with his despair. It seems as if all human experience has passed through him, and now there is nothing left in this world that could make him cry.

III

She walks past the shops selling last year's wares: an old pair of shoes, a sack of sugar, a toy German Shepherd that winds up and barks. It sounds like an electric siren. Everyone is struggling now to make ends meet. Everyone is trying to make do. Anna cannot help but mull over how much everything has changed.

When the Russians first arrived, we fed them our last morsels of bread, our sausage, our stored potatoes and beans. Whatever we had became theirs. The Germans had received news of the Soviet Army's approach before their arrival in January of '45, so the majority of Nazi soldiers had left Kraków for the west by that time. A few Nazis remained. The Soviet army did take prisoners of war, especially those who had been Gestapo or SS, and there were some executions, in a nearby village, but it was almost impossible to see a Nazi's body on the streets of our town. It did happen sometimes, though. There was an occasional fight with a soldier, a traitor, or a collaborator. There was an explosion caused by some Nazi soldiers that took place on a bridge away from the Wisła River. The possessions of those dead soldiers became fair game. There were boots, watches, shirts to be taken. People needed clothes. Here was a portrait of humanity that would not be easy to forget. Not only war can instill fear in a person's heart. Life is better without war, yes, but I cannot help but wonder what is yet to come.

Anna stops her internal rant to admire a small ornate opal pin in a shop window. The pin is a simple gold line dotted with tiny opals that form the points on a delicate star. Anna would like to own something like this. She imagines herself wearing a new dress made of fuchsia silk, imagines walking into a dance, being admired by the handsomest man in the room. The store owner, a woman of about seventy, sits at a table in the back. Barely visible through the foggy pane of the storefront window, she leans against her left hand, staring into space, smoking a long brown cigarette with her right hand. Every thirty seconds her pursed lips take a puff. Like so many other people around, she looks sad, gray. This is the life that has descended upon their world. They are all lucky to be alive, yes, but what price does living through the war make you pay? Anna takes another painful step, and with that twinge returns the ramblings of her mind.

Before the war, life was one big party. My family lived in Łódź, had a big, beautiful house with paintings on the wall and a maid in the kitchen. We didn't know that our house would be robbed or that we would be threatened. We were still enjoying our summer vacation in a small country village when my father returned to Łódź to gather some papers, only to find that Germans had broken into our home, stolen all our belongings, and even burned much of our house to the ground. We never went back.

Before the war, I was a girl of fourteen. We lived in a big comfortable home, my mother, father, Wojtuś, and I. Wojtuś is six years younger than me. Mama had him just when she thought that she couldn't have babies anymore. There he appeared, and so we all loved him the most, like he was our little doll. Wojtuś even looked like a doll, so pretty and delicate with his little blond curls and big blue eyes. Where I was a moody troublemaker, he was polite and kind. I remember once a beggar came to our house, and Wojtuś stopped the game he was playing in order to open the gate for the beggar, even helping him to pick the finest apples off the tree. Someone else's father would have given his child a scolding for what he did, but our father just laughed and picked Wojtuś up in the air, swinging him around with joy.

Not understanding the fuss he had caused, Wojtuś began to cry, tears spouting from his sweet innocent eyes.

"That's okay, dear Wojtuś," my father said, laughing, "We can have one less apple pie this year."

Every day my mother gave me a warm, buttered roll wrapped in foil for school, and every day as I reached the corner of our street I would throw the roll into the trash, smiling with the secret joy of knowing that I didn't have to eat it and that nobody would ever know what I had done. During the war, every day that I was hungry I thought about that buttered roll. Even now my mouth waters. If I knew then what I know now, things could have been different.

My hair has always been this stormy shade of black and blue, and my eyes have always been this dark. I was born blond just like the rest of my family, but I became ill when I was only four and had all of my hair shaved off. I didn't cry or blink an eye. I remember it like it was yesterday—I simply observed myself with grave consideration, watching my golden locks as they dropped slowly to the ground. With my solemn face and dark eyes, I resembled one of the old portraits hanging on the wall in the town library. My smile was so infrequent and surprising that when it did happen, everyone stopped to look. Even dinner got cold.

"Do it in circles," I demanded of my mother the time she shaved my head. She stood behind the old stuffed chair, razor in hand. I remember sitting before her, wrapped in a white cotton sheet, staring at my reflection in her ornate vanity mirror, tiny brown shoulders exposed, posture alert. "I want it to come back black and blue." Somehow my wish came true, and it was then that I imagined I might be a witch.

By the time I was five, I was well and had beautiful thick, dark curly hair.

Somehow everyone picked up on my strange capacity for sorcery, and everyone would tease me and call me a witch.

"That's right," I would joke, "I am a witch and you had better watch out, or else I will cast a spell on you." I could sense that even though everyone was friendly with me, they were also always a little bit afraid. I took pleasure in frightening my teachers, spouting nonsensical words, imitating black magic invocations. My teachers and my friends enjoyed these games, however slightly unnerving they might have been.

Of course since the war came, my abilities seem farther and farther away. Now I find myself thinking only of things: shoes, blouses, skirts, hats, coats, bras and panties, potatoes and bread. I never imagined that my life could become so mundane. But I remember when I was still a child and we had so much fun. I was the teacher's pet. I was their mistress of the occult, their Catholic girl, their dark horse in a sea of once and forever night.

My best friend, Rachelka, was also an unusual girl. She wore her long black curly hair in plaits that wrapped around her head like a rope on the dock of the black sea. Those ropes were like coiled snakes waiting to be provoked, unraveled, and drawn out into the murky waters of an unconquered world. She was like Rapunzel's dark sister, only she did not let down her golden hair, but rather collected her black silky locks and kept them to herself, creating the look of a child in an old woman's body, just waiting to be set free.

Rachelka was known by all our teachers as the special one in the group. She passed all of her lessons without effort, sang like an angel, and was a gifted painter. Everyone knew that one day soon she would become a great artist. Rachelka knew this about herself as well. She believed in her own bright future the way most young girls know for certain that they will become brides, mothers, have a house all their own. Their sheer confidence even allows them to imagine how many children they will have, and whether those kids will be boys or girls.

All of the students in the Mikolajskiej School for Girls were Jewish except for myself and three other girls. Why did our parents send us to a mostly Jewish school? Who knows? Maybe because it was the best school around. Things were not so separate then. Just because most of the students were Jewish doesn't mean that there was much of a difference between us. We all wore the same pleated gray skirt and starched white shirt. We studied the same maps, had our first periods, attended class trips, ate the same foods. Rachelka was the neighbor of Małgosia, whose father was in business with Malwina's uncle. Their mothers shopped at the same grocer, but not at the same butcher. Most girls went to temple, a few of us went to church. Our differences were small and almost unnoticeable.

The teachers at our school were mostly Catholic, though it was common knowledge that the beautiful and graceful young history teacher, Pani Tarkowska, came from a poor Jewish family in a nearby town. She wore long skirts and silk blouses in bright, friendly colors, but she could not hide her youth or her beauty. She was set to marry one of the most successful young merchants in Łódź—the son of a banker and a self-made businessman. Her eyes were bright with possibility.

Anna walks across the town square into St. Mary's Church, where she lights a candle, kneeling on the cold stones, staring up at the son of God.

Anna wonders if Jesus was really a man who existed in this world or if he is just a myth, an ideal man. Was what he suffered so different from what many people endured? Anna never was the type to go to church unless her parents forced her to, but now, ever since the war ended, she finds that it brings her some comfort, and comfort is hard to come by. She thinks of all those girls, her classmates from school, of how such a tiny difference in background could shape their whole world.

She didn't want to hear it, but he told her. Her kind father's face has taken a blow since the war, and now his skin looks waxy, as if he were quickly turning to stone.

"I want you to know, to understand, how lucky we are," he said, and then he told her what had happened. How her entire class, along with one or two younger students, had been locked in a tool shed behind the school, and then burnt to the ground.

"How do you know that?" Anna shouted, her face burning with rage, covering her ears in desperation, trying to block out a truth that cannot be ignored. And the ringing was so loud, as if upon hearing her scream the girls could finally scream, too, all at once. The heavens were in her ears, resounding with their call.

"No!" she cried, and fell to the table, hitting her forehead as she wept.

"But it is," her father said, softening, sitting beside her now, stroking her hair. "Everyone else was put in the ghetto, taken to the camps."

She had known without really knowing. Something had gone quiet at the start of the war, as if the memory of the girls' distant laughter were fading away. With that feeling came both terror and inner peace, a calm that was now wiped away by the spoken truth, by reality. Gone was the last bit of peace inside.

Even though she hadn't eaten enough soup that day to satiate her hunger, Anna still ran to the toilet and threw up what little was there. Never before was hunger so irrelevant as it was now, seated at her family table.

IV

Elżbieta makes a habit of collecting and hiding things. Clothes, books, old newspaper clippings. And what about drying the orange rinds to make a fire? She washes and presses her second-hand goods and locks them up in an old wooden wardrobe.

"For later," she tells herself, envisioning just how she will look while dancing in this dress or that shirt. There is nothing more valuable than clothing made of beautiful, fine silk and a ring made of real gold. When the mourning for her father passes (oh, when will it ever pass?), when the family gets back on its feet, when food becomes more easily available, she will be able to dance once more.

Baby Mateusz sleeps peacefully in his basinet while Waleria grates raw potatoes to make *czarne kluski* in the kitchen. Food is hard to come by these days, especially in the region of Silesia, and whenever a shipment arrives from the UNRRA, the United Nations Relief and Rehabilitation Administration, everyone runs to the township office to get his or her share. First the food goes to the Russian soldiers and then to everyone else. Elżbieta's siblings are out in the garden feeding the chickens. She can hear their cheerful shouts as they run from one another, darting between the old apple trees. Elżbieta's husband is out at school.

Sitting down in an old rocking chair to mend a pair of her little brother's socks, Elżbieta hums a tune to herself, an old Christmas carol that recalls the happy memories of her childhood. Maybe they didn't have much, but life was filled with joy. Their house was a home filled with love. And every summer her cousin Helena would bring Elżbieta to her *zameczek*—her little castle—in the countryside, where Helena lived with her husband, a Viennese nobleman who had horses and an endless stretch of land. It was here that Elżbieta was provided with painting and music lessons, where she danced and had her first kiss. Here she also became her ladyship, but just for the summer months. Whenever she returned home to Rybnik, her title, and her pleasure, would fade into oblivion.

Her grandmother, Julia, would yell at her every time she went. "Don't you know?" she would shout, hands on her broad hips, pale blue eyes glimmering in the sun. "That this isn't real? They will destroy your life if you keep going there, imagining you will be like them. You will never have their life." This would always devastate Elżbieta, and she would run to bed, tears in her eyes. *What does she know?* Elżbieta would tell herself. *She can't imagine how important those times are for me.*

Julia was Elżbieta's paternal grandmother, and Wiktor's mother. She was a strong woman, even stronger than Wiktor's wife, Waleria, and she was, as discussed in secret, *cyganka* (whisper: *she was a Gypsy*).

Elżbieta didn't know. She didn't know that hiding the truth from yourself can be a dangerous game. She had no idea that concealing the Gypsy truth, the street where she came from, the realities of her daily life, could be harmful to her future. But she couldn't help but feel that she was the most refined member of her immediate family. If any one of them were to have a charmed destiny, it would be her.

And here she was, just a few years later. Who could have imagined that the war would come? Who could have foreseen that the life they had known would take such a turn and that so many dreams would be smothered in the cold, dark earth? That her beloved papa, dear sweet Wiktor, would meet a tragic end?

Elżbieta was only sixteen when the war began. One year into the war she was able to find work at a well-respected flower shop in town, and it was there that she spent her days counting the roses and the lily of the valley whenever May would come. Even though there was a war, spring still came, and with it arrived the most beautiful delicate blossoms of violets and tender white lily of the valley that would shake and tremble in the wind. Elżbieta would bind them into miniature bouquets, creating small bunches of flowers wrapped in leaves. They were still affordable to some.

She had finished school at the age of fourteen, and was studying to become a piano teacher until the war began. This was a job that she could imagine herself doing. This way she could always be clean, her auburn hair rolled back, just so, framing the curve of her ear, the cuff of her blouse undone, and then she would always be surrounded by music. . . .

Roses are red, white, pink, and yellow. Roses are glorious gifts of nature, starting small, narrow, and then expanding and opening to inform the whole world of their extraordinary beauty. They offer you solace in difficult times. They serve as a reminder that life can improve, that there is always sun lurking somewhere beyond the clouds.

Elżbieta's grandfather, Albert, was known for growing prize roses. At the age of five he traveled alone on the train for days to meet his mother and her new husband in Bavaria with nothing but a suitcase, a teddy bear, and a small placard hanging from his neck that read "Albert Kajzerek, Rybnik, Poland." Through his experiences in Munich with a nobleman stepfather, he learned about gardening and acquired many other hobbies. He was given opportunities to experience things that he never would have dreamt of had he stayed at home. He could build furniture, make shoes, and grow prize roses with ease.

Albert would grow up to be a rather small man in size, a big man in stature. His family liked to tease him with the nickname "little emperor." He worked in a factory that produced enamelware, weighing ore on weekdays. On Sundays he would dress in a three-piece suit and gold watch, and, awaking at six, he would go to church and then walk twenty kilometers to meet with a master gardener on a nearby estate. For hours on end these two men would sit on apple crates in the tool shed or on a bench under the shade of an old oak tree, drinking homemade wine from a large jug corked with newspaper, discussing the best way to till the soil, to keep plant-eating snails at bay, to cultivate the perfect, most fragrant roses.

Albert and his wife, Maria, had a garden so clean that you could eat from the soil. These were Waleria's parents, Elżbieta's grandparents on her mother's side. They lived down on the west end of Ulica Strzelecka, where they had a field, a vegetable patch, pear trees, even a small bridge over a pond beneath which floated pink water lilies. On this tiny plot of land everything was beautiful and serene, even the last wisps of wheat floating off the fields in the late day sun, taking comfort in the final waves of the August heat.

Maria kept a small drove of cows, and they produced milk so pure that it became popular among Rybnik's Jews. Maria gave her Jewish customers open accounts, and she used these accounts to trade with her customers for beautiful fabrics. As a result, she was always well-dressed, even in difficult times.

During the war, the roses in the flower shop brought back familiar memories of Elżbieta's grandparents' garden, which was still vibrant, though much diminished in those difficult times. The roses' fragrant beauty was Elżbieta's link to St. Thérèse—to prayer and to unbridled hope. Like a beautiful melody that came from the heart, the roses were a reminder of family life and of peace, of the love and cultivated beauty that surrounded her. The sweet smell of roses was a promise that life was not over. Happiness would come around again one day soon.

Spending her days amid that heady aroma was a pleasure for Elżbieta, except when an SS officer would come into the shop to buy flowers for a lover or for his wife.

One afternoon, while Elżbieta was working alone, a tall, handsome officer with closely cropped blond hair and a pronounced jaw bound in to buy two-dozen roses for his Polish mistress. Elżbieta took pleasure in arranging his bouquet, though something made her nervous about the man. He stood there, back toward her, hands clasped behind him, eyeing the street, breathing heavily. She supposed that with a body that tall and that strong one would need to breathe heavily to survive. She watched him flick a piece of lint from the zigzagged double "s" embroidered in his collar. Elżbieta noticed her own hands trembling as she tied the pale violet ribbon into a perfect bow.

"Done," she said, meekly, calculating the cost of the bouquet.

The officer turned around and handed her the money for the flowers, and as she gave him his change, he slapped her right hand down onto the counter, and held it there tight, looking into her eyes. She tried to squirm away, but he was too strong, and besides, she was mesmerized by his stare.

"Don't you use soap?" he asked, face still, emotionless. "You'd better wash your eyes." And then he let go her hand, and left the store as loudly as he had come in.

As the door shut behind the officer, Elżbieta turned to look in the mirror at the back of the store. She looked just like any other Silesian woman, light hair, clear skin, pronounced nose, narrow lips. She was the prettiest of her sisters, but she did have eyes as black as a void.

That night Elżbieta had nightmares that she was in the forest at night and a black vulture was trying to scratch her eyes out. For weeks she would tremble like a frightened dog.

"Please don't go. Don't leave me alone," she would say to Pani Malik, her young boss, whose husband was off at war. "Don't be silly, my dear, you will be fine," Mrs. Malik would reply, stepping out of the store.

Little did Elżbieta know that it was Malik who was having the secret affair with the same SS officer who had threatened her just weeks earlier.

That year, Elżbieta would lose all of her teeth, one by one. The doctor said she was lacking in calcium, but it was the fear that stole away her youth.

V

If I could sell this pill on the black market I would, but I know that people have a difficult time seeing the possibilities in small items. They lack imagination, or at least that is what my father used to say. He sold watches, restored old clocks until they shined like new. He knew what was valuable and what wasn't, but he was always disappointed when other people couldn't see things the way he saw them. Whenever I see something old and beautiful and hidden, I think of him.

If I could sell this pill on the black market I would, but since I can't, I sell stockings, sugar, and sometimes perfume. Whatever I can get my hands on. Everything is in demand. Cigarettes are the easiest item to deal with, but there are so many other people doing the same business as me that I am always looking for new items to sell.

Once, sometime last autumn, a lady, a really nice lady, all dressed up with golden paint in her hair and a fur stole around her shoulders, came up to me in the street. I was standing near the Rynek by a small street, Ulica Św. Marka. I was looking through a garbage can because I hadn't eaten for two days and was starting to get very miserable. I knew that some nuns lived close to that corner, and once or twice I found a carefully placed sandwich in that can, as if it were there just for me, as if the pill were working its magic all over the place.

This lady saw me, I think, rustling through the can. I have to tell you that she was beautiful, the most elegant lady I had ever seen, and when she began talking to me, I felt so scared I wanted to run. I can't say I was ashamed. Two or three years ago I might have been embarrassed to be caught in such a situation, or at least I still imagined I could be, but since the war ended, things have been different. But still, this lady made me feel nervous, like I was going to get into trouble or something. Her voice was soft but stern. She told me not to run away.

"I will take you to *obiad* (lunch)," she said, and then announced, "Follow me."

I was so hungry I walked two steps behind her to hide the sounds of my hunger pangs the whole way. We passed through the market square and went downstairs into one of two restaurants in the center of town. There was a big room with painted windows that looked out onto the street and sent rainbows inside, just like they do in church. People think that light is God.

We sat at a big table with linen tablecloths, cloth napkins, and real silverware. I thought hard about taking a few knives and forks, shoving them in my pocket: that would have earned me some real money—the kind of money that could buy me a coat and some new shoes, even more dinners like this—but if I stole here, now, then I really wouldn't be worth the life that I was spared, so I thought better of it, even held my hands down under my legs beneath the table when I had to.

For five years all I had eaten was bread, potatoes, carrots and whatever apples I could find. Once I had *naleśniki*. But on this unbelievable day I ate two kinds of pierogi, young potatoes, green beans, veal cutlet, and for dessert, wild strawberries the size of ladybugs, mixed with fresh cream. I swayed to the exhilarating sensation of tasty food—something I had nearly given up on. As the light poured in from the window in beams of blue, red, and yellow, I swooned. The lady told me that she was from Warsaw. She was an actress, which made sense, because she was so beautiful. She looked like an angel. When my stomach was filled, for a moment I thought that I saw stars in her eyes. "Could it be?" I asked myself. The magic? The pill? As if heaven itself had come down to earth to sit at my table, to surround my little world.

I could tell that the waiters weren't too happy about having me there, but I tried not to care. I wasn't too clean that day either. I hadn't had a haircut in months. I tried to cut it myself with some old scissors I found in an abandoned factory—the one where all those young women died, the one people tell stories about, where the girls decided to end their lives together, all at once. But with just a shard of glass to use as a mirror, I didn't get very far.

That factory was a very nice place to stay, I have to say, even though it was haunted by the spirits of those dead girls. This whole town is inhabited by ghosts, anyway, so who cares? Even if you think you are in the cleanest place, living like a king, there is no escaping their memory. I liked sleeping in that old workroom for a time. The war was over, and I felt free once again. I didn't have to hide in the train station anymore; I could begin to live. There was a feeling of warmth in the room that can't be found in most old buildings in Kraków, and the machines had a certain comforting odor, like a mixture of oil and soap. Maybe that was the leftover girly smell.

One day I realized it might not be such a good idea to live with just a group of lost souls, even if it was so comforting to me. Living with the dead can be dangerous. That isn't just a fairytale, you know. Spending too much time with them can make you lose sight of the border between worlds, and then you never can predict on which side you'll get caught. Besides, those girls might not really want me around—they could have things to do, people to meet on the other side.

So a couple of months ago my life changed when I found a room with an old blind lady who still lives in Kazimierz. She took pity on me because she lost all three of her sons during the war, and she wanted to save just one lost boy.

"Just one," I heard her whisper to herself, standing in the hallway the first time I walked out the door. She let me live with her for free, and I helped her with the shopping, the cleaning, and the cooking. Living in her house meant I could even take a bath once a week. I didn't need the magic pill like I used to, which is partly why

I am showing it to you, because it is important to share, because I can see that you too need rescuing.

For a while I was really feeling like life was on my side once again. I could see a future, and it looked bright. I walked along the Wisła River at night and smiled. The earliest signs of spring were coming; I could feel the moon looking down on me and I would look right back up at it. I felt like saying, "*You* did it, moon. I know you did."

Spring is so beautiful in Kraków that it is easy to forget that winter ever existed, as if it would never come around again. You hide your heart from the deep freeze, from the cold.

Two weeks ago the old lady got very sick. I woke up one morning to find her doubled over on the kitchen floor. A neighbor helped me carry her to the hospital. Now I am without a place to sleep again until she comes back home. I hope she comes back. I have returned to sleeping in the train station, or when nights are warm like this I roll out some newspaper (it has so many uses!) in Planty or by the river, and I lie down under the stars. In the evening I go and visit the old lady in the hospital, but these last few days she hasn't looked so good. I still have hope she'll get better. The pill helps me to believe in so many things. I know my hope won't help to keep her in this world. I learned that a long time ago. She wouldn't be the first Polish woman to ever lose her life to heartbreak.

VI

He was the first young man Elżbieta met after the war who looked clean-shaven. His broad forehead with the widow's peak and thick, dark hair, together with his serious expression, called to mind the perfect picture of an elegant man. He may not have had a lot of money, but his suit was still made of fine, hand-tailored wool. He still wore in his lapel a tiny white spray rose. Twenty years later Elżbieta would see the portrait of a great French writer—an aviator who wrote a children's book her son would use as the text for the audition that got him accepted into the Warsaw drama school (the French writer's name sounded like Expray)—who would also remind her of him. The photo would confirm something that she felt deeply, that this was an elegant man, the sort of man a lady such as herself should have in her life.

During the war, many of Rybnik's young men, boys fresh as sixteen, were taken into the Wehrmacht, the German army at the time, to serve the Third Reich. Rybnik was a town inside Upper Silesia, a region of Poland that was German up until 1921, when the League of Nations organized a border referendum and the Second Polish Republic was established. Suddenly Upper Silesia was Poland again, and depending on where a person came from one could feel more Polish or more German. Brothers were torn apart over this issue of national identity. Families fought constantly, and the region saw three bloody uprisings. Assimilated Jews who considered themselves German left Rybnik in large numbers when it was declared Poland, only to be replaced by Jews from other parts of the country, Jews who were less acceptable to the local population. Several assimilated families did stay behind. They did not feel so much German as they felt themselves to be citizens of Rybnik.

When the war began and Silesia was occupied by the Germans, most Silesian boys were still considered German, depending on the area they lived in, and could therefore be drafted into the war. Though they weren't SS men, they wore uniforms with the symbol of the German army on their jackets, consisting of an eagle with a swastika at its feet. Though many of them resisted, they still saluted the Fuhrer. They were, in effect, German soldiers.

Some boys went to Russia while others were stationed in Italy or France. Some were expected to do things that were brutal, painful, that supported the Nazi agenda, though it was understood that the Wehrmacht did not hold the same kind of destructive power as the security service, the SS.

Elżbieta's friend, Bernard, who had studied French, recalled being stationed in the south of France. He was quietly guarding a post when he overheard two French soldiers talking behind him. They were chewing tobacco and looking out over the sea.

"The Germans will never win with boys like that fighting for them," he overheard the older soldier saying. The younger soldier grunted in agreement. Bernard crouched down. He was only seventeen.

Elżbieta's husband, Bolesław, was eighteen when the war broke out. The Germans planned to take him to Stalingrad, and he had only two days to say goodbye to his family and prepare for departure. For the rest of his life Bolesław would recall the night before he was to leave. He lay quietly in bed, still as a mouse, and the more motionless he became, the more agitated he felt. His older sister, Wanda, was snoring in the room across the hall, the full moon pouring into her bedroom through lace curtains, casting the apartment in a cold blue light. He felt as if the moon were taking over the world. He was too young to lose this battle with life.

I will lose. Never will I make love to a girl, never toast a friend's wedding. I will lose.

He would forever recall the shouts that emanated from the kitchen. He could hear his mother begging and pleading with his father for hours, but Bolesław couldn't decipher what was being said.

The next morning, at the crack of dawn, she threw on her coat and covered her head with a scarf, and ran uphill to the church. She begged Mother Mary to take care of her beloved son, promising her everything, lit a candle, standing very still until she could see the flame rising, dancing in the cold, damp air, and then she walked straight down the hill, right into Nazi headquarters (also known as the town hall). Shaking on the inside, she asked to speak with the highest-ranking officer, and once she was inside his office with the door shut, she removed from the lining of her coat three Viennese paintings rolled up into a single narrow tube. The paintings were masterfully executed and valuable, worth more money than a year's salary for the handsome young officer.

He took them gently into his hands, unrolled them onto his massive oak desk, and glanced at them with a satisfied smile. He then proceeded to roll them tenderly back up. He looked up at the woman, seemingly calm and at ease. He noticed the fine wool of her coat, the delicate curls of her dark hair, pinned up beneath a floral-printed scarf. She was not unlike so many proud middle-class women in Germany.

The corners of her mouth twitched a little, but she was unable to smile. She simply stood before him, hands clasped, waiting for a reply.

"Stalingrad is no place for a young and talented boy such as your son," the officer smiled and nodded his head. "We have soldiers stationed in Norway, above Bergen. This will be a much better place for him to spend his time."

Her solid thank you and swift departure felt like a dream. Hidden waves of sweat poured from her body as she bowed to the officer and left the room as quickly as possible. When she reached the corner of the town square and was certain that nobody from the headquarters could see her, she hid beneath a small archway, leaned her hot cheek against the wall, and wept like a baby. Relief is like a tidal wave. It hits you at the strangest moments, and with it often comes the endless well of your deepest, hidden sorrow.

Bolesław would live. He had always wanted to become a lawyer, but he would wind up a bookkeeper, first working in agriculture, and later in the coal mines. He did go to Norway, one of several boys from his region. He excelled at skiing, and so was put to work transporting mail on skis from one post to another. These were the most beautiful moments, when he could imagine that he was free, that there was no war, when he would fly down a mountain or stop to take photos of the distant horizon. He was also given a post guarding French prisoners of war. Sometimes there were aerial attacks, but mostly things remained calm up there in the mountains above Bergen. So many lonely nights, yes, and days when he hid in the barracks and cried for the pain of missing his mother, his father, and even his sister, Wanda, who had always only cared about herself.

VII

When I take this pill, I feel all quiet inside. Then I know that there are no whispers crawling down into my heart at night. No ghosts to disturb my mind. Here is the cemetery where nobody goes. See that mausoleum over there? It's a good place to hide for an hour or two. You can fit your body, if you are small enough, between the headstone and the overgrown grass. The tall green blades may scrape your ankles and your elbows, but they smell so fresh, as if nothing bad could ever happen to you there. And that is the best place to disappear.

I want to tell you something, but don't tell anybody else, okay? There is a woman here. The first time I saw her was out of the corner of my eye, like a shadow passing beneath the bridge near Wawel Castle, but then I saw her whole figure tracing the paths between gravestones. She has been here for two days already. She didn't notice me, but I saw her wandering through the cemetery and through Kazimierz at night. It's like she's looking for somebody.

I tried calling out to her, but she just kept mumbling to herself, pulling on her long gray skirts and weeping. I can't understand how she can cry so much. I have no more tears to shed.

"Can I help you, lady?" I ask, but she doesn't hear me at all. I wish I knew just what she was looking for. I could help her if only she could hear me or see me.

Sometimes even with the pill I can't seem to get through the day without feeling this dark emptiness creep in. There is a sinking feeling that comes upon me without warning—as if I am drowning in a sea noticeable only to me, as if the waters of invisibility are surrounding me. For the rest of the world it looks like I am just a boy standing on the street, but for me it is hard to breathe. "Don't take me," I whisper to the darkness. First it beckons, and then it recedes.

One night last winter there was a commotion over on Bożego Ciała, not far from the church on the corner. I was crossing Plac Wolnica on my way to the river to sleep when I heard shouting and the sound of glass breaking, so I ran back down the street and hid in the churchyard of the bazylika, next to an old, burnt-out lamppost. I stayed still all night, and I am pretty sure my breath never even made a sound.

Two people were murdered in their apartment that night. The papers called this an "incident." Things like this happen all the time but nobody seems to talk about them anymore.

Sometimes I wonder if I am becoming invisible. Everyone who knew me and loved me is gone. First there was death, and then there weren't any people anymore. Now there are new people who want to forget that the old people were ever there. But there is a different kind of flower that is sprouting on the ghetto side of the river. Maybe my pill is changing shape and someday the earth will grow plants to make everything right in the world. I will be first in line to celebrate when that day comes.

VIII

On his wedding day just four months after the war was over, Bolesław refused to have his picture taken. He who had passed the time while in the Norwegian fjords photographing mountains and lakes could not bring himself to immortalize this one crucial moment. "Later, later," he told Elżbieta, as he would continue to do for the next forty years, putting her off as he always would from savoring her pleasure.

From now on, whenever she wanted to make sacred what was beautiful, he would always complain.

This was an invisible line written on their wedding certificate. And so it was. Some vows remain silent.

Now there was a new generation of frightened, masculine men to contend with. To care for a dog, an orchard, a few hens, that was safe, but to love a person, that was an altogether different story. Going to war had frozen the hearts of so many boys. Leaving Mama—the comfort of her clean home, the baked bread and the churning of butter that turned into the war machine of death and confused innocent minds that had no time to differentiate between one world and another—was a killer to the childlike soul. And in those endless days, bowels opened and memories became vibrant. Men sat and waited.

Memories of fresh linens hanging on the lines behind their mothers' houses cast endlessly wet days in the forests and the trenches in a faint light of hope. Bodies no longer living were wrapped in wide muddy sheets. While men watched their friends being rolled up like carp in today's newspaper ready to be cooked for Christmas Eve dinner, their hair matted with blood and mud, onlookers turned away from the lifeless image and chose memory. They smelled the sweet divine call of Mama's fresh apple cake and remembered home. If Mama were here she would lift that sheet, suddenly spotless, suspend it with her line between these two trees, and with her tender touch, her aching heart, the lifeless body would rise and become new again.

All those crucified futures still hang in the atmosphere like mist. I can see it now, from golden autumn until early spring. I hear it whistle in the faint rustle of life as the wind passes through wet molecules that hover effortlessly in the air. They smell like distant smoke. Somewhere in the wet grassy dew there is a fire smoldering, a childhood dream that was never extinguished. If you listen carefully, ear to air, you can hear all those little boys, hearts crying, smothered and alone in this silence that blankets the world with its memory.

IX

And now there are men like this:

Karol, who wanted to become a priest just so he could wear those beautiful velvet vestments, and day in day out stare at the beams of light as they played shadow games across the stained glass windows, hypnotizing him. Frankincense and myrrh and the heady imaginings of devotion—serving someone so great that he could never be found. Karol, who saw so many friends die before him en route to France that he decided never to count on people again. Life was too unreliable for him. Money and possessions were a much safer bet, and drink helped him forget. There was a dimension to this world that he would prefer not to know, but now he knew, and a gold chain on his dead friend's neck now carried a monetary value that meant more to him than the sentimental desires of any poor mother's heart.

X

Up here the world looks so different than it does down there. Through the stars I can see a tiny white globe in the distance, and I recognize it as the place where I have been before and where I will go again. Soon. And oh, little feather, I don't really want to go.

My little feather laughs as if to assure me that I will never be alone anyway.

If only people down there knew what my feather knows, then they could see through their veil of tears.

XI

Not since the war ended had Elżbieta felt so beautiful as she did on that golden September day. The weather was occasion to smile. It was a sign of happier days to come. Her auburn hair was pulled back at the temples with small green enamel clips and tiny white baby's breath buds attached at the ends. Her dress was made of fine black silk. At the left tip of the collar and hidden within the asymmetrical pleat on her right leg was an embroidered black rose. If you could see an x-ray portrait of her heart, you would find another rose flowering there, one color for every season.

If Elżbieta were to dance, then the black rose would be exposed, displayed to the world and released from its hiding place. But that never happened, especially on this day.

There were things other than the black embroidered rose concealed by her dress. There was a new life growing and stirring inside her, three months to the day. This baby may have been conceived out of wedlock, but it didn't matter. He would be brought into this world with love. Though Wiktor had offered Bolesław a way out, saying that he would take responsibility for the unborn child, Bolesław decided to do the right thing, to marry the delicate and charming young Elżbieta, to learn to be a husband and to love.

In her short life Elżbieta had seen babies born and even seen babies die, but never had she considered what it would feel like to have one growing inside her. There was a rustling of subtle movement, a wave of ocean within, and such an ecstatic joy to experiencing this fertile ground, to looking out at the vast garden behind her grandparents' home, watching summer's end as evidenced in the bounty of vegetables pulled from the earth, and knowing that, inside her, a kind of harvest was also taking place. Inside there was water, inside there was sun, and inside there was also purest, sweetest life.

At this moment she did not know that even though the war was over, life would continue to take from her many of the people whom she loved, that life was still life. But to Saint Thérèse she could whisper, now and always, *What sweet child grows inside? Take care to bless him with your goodness, to keep him healthy and safe and warm. Take care, Saint Thérèse. Shower him with your roses. May no harm come to him.* And it never did.

Elżbieta had never imagined this excitement nor could she envision the accompanying goodbye. This whisper: so long to dreams of a better life, to sitting at the piano with a student, to knowing more. Yet at this moment, standing at the altar of the tiny chapel with Bolesław by her side, the growing child in her stomach, her mother and father, sisters and brother, the golden autumn in full swing, and the late-day sun pouring through the red and yellow stained glass windows, casting a halo of light above the sculpted head of Christ, she knew that she could happily accept that what she had was enough. Rybnik was her home, and this new family was her life. If only she could memorialize this moment and take a picture. But she never would.

XII

Now that she was an adult, Anna wished she had never been a witch as a child. Witches are smart. They know too much, and if they are true to themselves, they grow up to become wild.

Every morning at daybreak she would climb the stone walkway and enter the gates of Wawel Castle, showing her papers first to one soldier and then to another.

During the war, her dreams were overpowered by images of her old schoolmates, especially Rachelka, who seemed to be everywhere she turned. Rachelka's image even floated below the Wisła River's surface, her pale, thoughtful face mounting an endless stream of water, facing the sky for all time.

In dreams Anna envisioned herself playing in the garden behind her old house, even dancing with a young soldier in the pale moonlight. She climbed Mount Everest, and just as she was about to reach its summit she knelt carefully in the snow, removing a tiny Polish flag from the frozen corners of her coat pocket. There was Rachelka, alone and naked in a quiet snowdrift. She didn't speak to Anna at all, only closed her eyes and leaned back, frost decorating her hair like crystal balls dangling from the mangled branches of an old tree.

In visions and in dreams. How many times did she have nightmares in which faces were measured, analyzed, condemned?

Black hair and dark eyes. Oversize noses and heads. Children being beaten by tall, handsome soldiers. Hungry maggots devouring bodies with delight.

Black hair and dark eyes aren't everything. The Gypsy, the Jew, the unknown stranger. The nose whose tip leans toward the sky like a flower opening to the sun, this is the one that protects you from a desperate fate. But some noses are tricky, don't you think? So many Polish faces cross that line, and yet you say that you always know. But it isn't just the nose, you say. A Jew is a Jew is a Jew, right?

And then there is the dream that repeats and extinguishes all others. In this dream, it is always night. There is a large, burnt-out building in the middle of an empty city where even the darkest corners are shadowed by the moon. Three young girls, strangers, play a game in which they sing and dance in a circle, holding hands in the pale, white light. They sit in the empty yard building sculptures out of dirt. They make furniture and dolls and play house, the starched white collars of their uniform shirts dirtied from layers of soot and soil. Anna reaches out to touch one girl's shoulder, and it crumbles beneath her hand. Everyone disappears. She is left only with a dark, empty house.

In an instant she is on a train moving away from the city into the countryside, two newborn lambs by her side. One of them is crying for its mother, and whenever she tries to offer him comfort, he just cries louder, tears big enough to fill a glass slipping between the wooden slats of the train car's door, stretching wide before the vast green world, falling into the passing landscape, disappearing down into the forbidden, fertile earth.

XIII

Anna had only just arrived in Kraków when the streets were renamed. Even the town square was now called Adolf Hitler Platz. As if the country had been stolen from itself, now hiding until the storm would pass. And what if it never did? Then Polish words would be absorbed deep into the earth, sounds blurred and covered. Murmurs emitted in this language built for secrets. These sounds, they roll off the tongue like an endless whisper.

The governor-general of occupied Poland had chosen Kraków as his home base, in part due to the city's Germanic flare. *So much beauty here,* he said to himself and to his many colleagues. Such opportunity. So, so many Jews. The Jewish population made up roughly a quarter of the city's population, and so he fantasized about what their removal could do for this otherwise beautiful town. There was a plan set in motion, though it would never be completely fulfilled. Men stood at his altar, and whatever he said, went.

Niklas might have been the last man you would imagine to be found working under such a high ranking-official, but here he was, sleeping in a room in Wawel Castle, overlooking the Wisła River, which ran through this beautiful city of Kraków, drifting past the ghetto walls, rough within and perfect without.

Raised in a small German town in the north, he had never left his village until Hitler came to power. He couldn't even read or write, but it was his skill for sweet-talking, his talent for charming people, that helped him to move quickly through the ranks of the new regime. First a local landowner sent him into the Wehrmacht as a soldier, and, before long, Niklas became a close confidant of the governor-general of occupied Poland. This job suited him better than any other he could have ever imagined. It looked clean and respectable on the outside, but there was still plenty of dirty work involved. Having lived the majority of his life isolated on a farm, Niklas had raised countless herds of cows, honing his skills, learning the best ways to care for and fatten the animals before slaughter. He was made for this work.

Though he had spent so much of his young life alone with his parents on the farm, Niklas had a way with people that was unmatched. It was as if he could see into them, identify their greatest fears and their greatest desires, and from that point of understanding, anything was possible.

As a child, he was terrified every time his father prepared the animals for slaughter, but as he grew older and became man of the house, he came to enjoy the contrasts of building life up only to tear it down. There was nothing like the feeling of raising an animal, knowing all along that whenever he wanted, he could simply kill it with a single blow. There was an unknown pleasure that he experienced when encountering another being's fear. This was power, he long ago realized, an excitement like none other he had ever known.

It all made perfect sense now, Niklas thought, stretching his tan arms in the early morning sun. A faint haze was rising over the river on this summer morning, just as it often did until the strong afternoon light could penetrate the seemingly ever-present soft pink fog. Then there would be a stunning clarity to the day that would last until early evening, when the miasma would descend across the city once again. Kraków was like a dream.

His time on the farm, his father's brutality whenever he made a mistake with the animals or the barn, the thrashings that he took as a child, they all helped him to become the man he was today. And when his father beat his mother, calling her names and forcing her to clean on her hands and knees, Niklas learned to fight his weaknesses and resist the temptations of the heart. He learned quickly that it didn't pay to feel attached to anyone. He tried to stay close to the cycles of life. It was strangely comforting to accept the fact that death was always on the other side.

And when his father died, he wept like a baby, hiding inside the linen closet for days. His mother implored him to open the door, take a drink, eat a little bread, but Niklas adamantly refused. When he came out, he was a different man. He made certain that from that point on, nothing would ever make him cry again.

XIV

It was too late for Anna to go back once the job had begun. She thought about it more than once, about leaving the whole thing behind, but she could never move herself to do it. She felt she had no choice. At least this way she could help out her father, support her mother and Wojtuś in the countryside, buy real stockings with a seam up the back.

She had lived in Kraków for only one week when she began working for the Nazi Party. She was hired first as a secretary in town, in part because she was young and pretty, but also because her German was excellent. Here was one advantage of growing up in multicultural Łódź. Now was the time to boast one's German-language skills and to conceal one's knowledge of Yiddish. Less than two years later Anna was given a job cleaning in Wawel Castle. She would stay for one year before returning to work in town. It didn't matter, she told herself one sunny day, while passing a gang of young Polish laborers standing on the street in their Baudienst uniforms. This was just a moment in time, another step on Poland's road to nowhere. She had become a member of the lost herd, working to survive. Never in her life would she admit to another human being just how grateful she was for the distraction, despite her absolute hatred of the job, the people, the cheap uniform. Why had she gotten the job? Why, out of all of the beautiful and smart and stupid candidates, had she been chosen to have more money— to clean the desks, to make the coffee, to be very still, to listen and to obey? Where was the happiness in luck? In being the chosen one? Why is any witch ever given an advantage over any other? No, sometimes Anna wished she had never, ever begun.

Every morning she would wake up earlier than she had ever done for school. The strange half-light at this time of day reminded her of important holidays as a child. Those were the days when excitement pulled her body from sleep, and nothing could keep her down. Times were different now.

There were the long hours spent washing, folding, dusting, and cleaning the floors of marble staircases so grand that they could supply the whole world with heavenly imaginings. There was a grand ball, a room full of dancing couples, in her mind. It was a perfect gathering in which the past was resurrected; only now it would be better. Poles and Jews danced together, served by a German wait staff that wore white gloves to offset the pale marble staircase. They supplied drinks and said "yes" and "thank you" whenever necessary. Jewish women would display their dark, curly hair, and blond Polish dames would flatter them by saying, "Oh, if only my limp hair would do the same."

This was a game Anna played whenever she became really angry or bored, for in the world of her imagination she could do whatever she wanted with the German waiters, especially when she was in a particularly witchy mood. She could force them to wear masks that resembled pig snouts, push them to their knees, even use the most preciously designed riding crop normally reserved for the local nobleman's horse to whip them on their wild pony behinds while they served drinks.

As pretty as this ball may have been, as many exquisite dresses as may have been present, constructed like live replica confectionary delights—women as cream puffs and such—and as many lovely waltzes and handsome men may have offered her their perfect, most masculine hands, pulling her out onto the dance floor for "one last turn," Anna's imaginings were neither delicate nor kind. But they did help pass the time.

Days went like this: First she received orders from the Polish head housekeeper. Then she cleaned the hallways or the first floor with three young women and took a break for lunch. Finally the group split up to clean various parts of the castle. Although the governor-general and his family had a trusted staff of German servants (with exception of their house twenty kilometers outside of town, which was cared for mostly by Polish housekeepers), Anna and her friend Maryna—who, like her, spoke excellent German and was fifteen-years-old passing for seventeen—were chosen to clean for Niklas, the governor-general's close subordinate, as he lived on the Wisła River side of the estate, in a building away from the governor-general's home. This was the most interesting part of Anna's shift, because Niklas was almost never around, and the girls had some freedom to drift through the rooms and let their minds wander. Sometimes Anna played another game with herself, spying on him or snooping through his things. You could learn about people by searching through their possessions. Like how the boss folded the cuffs of his shirtsleeves just so, as if always preparing for perfection, as if life did not provide him with enough time to crease his shirt cuff in anticipation of . . . what? In the privacy of his castle, this monster became more like a man.

There were so many ways to see into a person's soul. Invisibility was the key to knowing another man's heart. Here, for the first time in her life (and never, ever to be repeated), Anna learned as best she could how to hide in the shadows. It took effort, but she found ways to achieve it. She pinned back her shiny black hair, slumped her shoulders (a habit that proved difficult to emerge from), wore no makeup, and donned the hausfrau uniform worn by all the other housekeepers. Hers was always at least one size too big.

Some days she worked on the boss's rooms, shining his shoes and lining up his white shirts so that there was not more than one centimeter's space left between each hanger. She had heard that Niklas's quirks were nothing compared to the governor-general's. He sometimes made his housekeepers rewash his one hundred uniforms in just one day. She also heard that he had a habit of obsessively cleaning his nails. Once he actually whipped his son for bringing a caterpillar into the bedroom. Yes, the governor-general's wife and children lived in the castle as well. They enjoyed lavish banquets prepared by an Austrian chef who had been imported from Vienna just for them. They spent weekends in a villa outside Kraków, where from the top of a hill they could see the rolling fields of Małopolska running away from them. The children played in forests and in streams. For them, life was beautiful.

Working at Wawel Castle at this time made Anna feel like a cloistered witness to the end of a world. It had ended already, in the destruction of her family home, in the door that had been closed on Łódź, in the train ride with her father from the countryside to Kraków, in the faces of her mother and Wojtuś as the family divided and went their separate ways. It ended in the crease that formed so early between her brows. But here in Wawel Castle, proud heritage sight for the Polish people, where the dragon's lair still rested beside the Wisła, the old world died. You could walk twenty minutes and see people being cordoned off, you could share a sandwich with Maryna, laugh with her or cry, you could tell her a secret, and tomorrow she could be gone.

Maryna's real name was Miriam. With her stunning green eyes and electric smile, day-by-day she lived a secret life. She had acquired documents stating that she was a Pole, and she lived with a Catholic family in town. When she changed her name, she learned Catholic prayers and did what she could to erase Jewish life from her memory. But you can't obliterate who you are. While she scrubbed the marble steps, her mother and sisters moved into the ghetto. On days when Maryna was dismissed early from work, she would visit her family using documents that endorsed her as a Polish nurse in the Apteka, one of the few places of gentile presence in the ghetto. She was able to keep this up until the first deportation, at which point access to the ghetto became more restricted, and the core group of nurses identifiable. But until the gates were closed she smuggled bread, medicine, and news.

There may have been a few other Jewish women cleaning at Wawel Castle, sweeping the walkways or scrubbing the façade. If there were, nobody really knew. Did they have work papers and live in the ghetto? Did they slide off their armbands and move from one world safely into the next? Were they, like Maryna, hiding out in town? Who was this woman? Who was the other? Who knows the truth of everyone's story? Even in an era of great restriction, there were always exceptions to every rule. And so many secrets. For always there was a Jew hiding in the light of day.

During this period of time, when she was new to Wawel and Maryna was often by her side, Anna vomited at least once a day. She would just go about her business, working, and then suddenly she would run to the toilet to retch. Luckily this only lasted for a few months and nobody ever knew about it, not even Maryna. Anna would have been ashamed for her to know. Maryna never complained about her circumstances, and the only possible evidence of her suffering came once a month when she experienced terrible period pain. Anna would always know that it was coming, because suddenly Maryna's face would take on the palest pallor and she would begin dropping things left and right. Once it was so bad that she fainted on the boss's bedroom floor. Anna dragged Maryna's body to the bathroom so she could pour cold water onto her face, but Maryna still bled heavily onto her uniform and onto the pale-yellow-carpeted floor. The two risked getting into trouble by spending an extra hour cleaning. Finally Anna tied a white apron backward around Maryna's uniform.

Their boss, Niklas, was not a good man by anyone's standards, but he was good at what he did. He once thrashed a dog to death on Wawel Square just for begging him for food. This event interrupted Niklas's address to a group of young soldiers. He said that the murder was meant to teach them all a lesson in obedience. Anna watched the whole thing from a courtyard window. She could see the excitement in his eyes.

Anna saw it all begin. It started when they were cleaning his sleeping quarters on a summer's day. The morning had been sunny and beautiful, but now that it was afternoon the sky was overcome with darkness and it began to storm. The head housekeeper came rushing into the room, hair wet and matted, apron undone, and told them to move on quickly. Niklas was on his way, and would want to enter his room in peace. So the girls, who had never even met him, quickly straightened the bed sheet corners.

They had just shut the massive bay windows (it took two girls to open or close just one) and began drying the floors when the door was thrown open and Niklas came rushing in. He had blood on his right hand and on his rain-soaked white shirt (he never wore a uniform), and he screamed for the girls to get out, while he marched into the bathroom and slammed the door. From their perch at the top of the stairs, they heard curses and the sound of glass breaking. They didn't know what to do or where to go, so they just sat there attentively. At first they were both trembling, but after a few minutes of silence they began to relax, Anna braiding Maryna's thick, chestnut hair. Minutes passed before Niklas stormed out of the room and down the stairs past them, marching wildly, his whole body tense and jumping as he walked, frightening the girls so much that Anna dropped the hairpin and watched it fall down the central spiral of the marble stairs. No one could hear that pin drop in the cacophony of sounds. There was the wild thunder barreling down on the city, which almost totally drowned out the sound of Niklas shouting at several SS guards, who were standing outside in the rain.

When Niklas came back upstairs, he was relaxed. He walked slowly up the stairs and even dared to smile, asking the girls if one of them could bring him some fresh soap and a towel. Anna ran to an adjacent building to get the things he requested, discreetly picking the hairpin off the floor as she went. It took her some time to find the kind of soap he liked, one that had no fragrance and was clear and brown, like the simple kind used for washing clothes. It must have been at least five minutes before Anna came back upstairs, because by this point Maryna was no longer sitting there.

The door to Niklas's room was ajar, but there was no one inside. The air was heavy, but Anna assumed it was a result of the dampness left over from the rain. The door to the bathroom was also slightly open, and in his dresser mirror Anna could see a reflection of the bathroom mirror. She was surprised by her own quiet response as she watched Maryna sit calmly on the edge of the tub. She did not breathe more quickly as she witnessed Maryna clean the wound on Niklas's hand and then bandage it with a strip of cloth that she must have ripped off of his shirt. She did not drop her things—the towel and the brown soap, as she watched him bow his head, as if in submission, and lean over to kiss Maryna on the lips. She did not quiver when she saw Maryna smile sweetly, or when Niklas turned to close the door, catching sight of Anna watching. She wondered if Maryna knew that there were tears in his eyes.

*

There is only one way to make pastry dough so that it is light and fluffy enough to bake. First you beat the eggs clockwise and then counterclockwise, and that way the result will be the most delicate and delightful cloud puffs you have ever eaten. This is Bolesław's role in the household on Saturday evenings, when he and Elżbieta bake a cake. He whips the eggs. He kneads the dough. Sometimes they make *szarlotka* (apple cake), and at other times, a chocolate torte, such as for birthdays or holidays. The rest of the time they make apple cake, or else Elżbieta's special cookies filled with rose-petal jam, which taste like a piece of heaven.

Elżbieta hums a tune remembered from her piano-playing days. It might be Chopin. On her face is the same secret smile that is always there. It is the smile evident in her eyebrows and in her lips, in the way that her cheeks turn upward, toward rosy thoughts and better days.

There is nothing like the smell of that jam as it fills the kitchen. When the aroma of apples and butter baking together hits the atmosphere there is a slight pause in life, and for a second there is familiarity, a feeling of coming home, a sensation that you were always there to begin with, no matter what has gone wrong. This smell is so evocative that it will forever recall childhood, family, and memory.

Looking up from her bowl of baking powder and sugar, Elżbieta glances over at Bolesław, who is sitting on a stool, hunched over a bowl of eggs, eyes cast downward, intent upon completing his task to perfection. He feels her looking, so he looks up at her and smiles, a break of sunlight that doesn't come to his face often, but when it does, it is always a miracle. Uncharacteristically, he grabs Elżbieta and pulls her onto his lap. The flour from her hands get all over his face and shirt, and together they laugh. They laugh and laugh, and, for this moment in time, everything is as it should be.

XV

Better not to remember the war, now that it is over, Anna reminds herself, walking down Ulica Sławkowska on her way to buy groceries. The old market has little to offer now, but there are things one can get, like potatoes and carrots, things that can help keep a person alive. Out of the corner of her eye she sees that same haunting little boy again, the one who was wandering the streets with another child just days ago. He is standing in Planty, carrying a little dog in his arms. This dog has all of the fat that the young boy lacks. He is old and scruffy, and his eyes look filmed over, as if they are almost blind. The little boy holds the dog close to his face, inhaling his fur, as if he will never let him go. A bearded man in a dark brown suit sitting on a nearby bench turns around to say something to the boy, and as if in response, the boy puts down the dog and the dog runs back to the man. The boy stands there, frozen, and the man says something to him again. The boy comes over to sit next to him.

Carrying a bag with a few necessities, Anna sees the boy again on her way home. This time she stops to really look. The hollows of his cheeks are just as sunken as they were before, and his hair is even wilder than it was. Eyes closed, he listens intently to the man. The man looks like a foreigner. He has a small bandage on the right side of his forehead. Occasionally he pauses to touch the plaster and shut his eyes. In these moments the boy looks away.

She decides to walk through Planty so that she can really observe them. She hears the man speaking to the boy in Yiddish. She cannot help but worry about him, at least a little. Maybe it isn't necessary anymore, but it is still an automatic response to want to tell them to hide who they really are. An elderly lady with a German Shepherd comes along, and the little dog gets excited and begins to jump up and down and bark. The little boy goes after him. The man on the bench holds his head as if in pain, probably in reaction to the sound. The little dog lifts his leg and begins to urinate on the large dog. Something more marvelous than the leg of lamb Anna has just purchased on the black market is the sight of this seemingly starving boy opening his mouth and howling with laughter. He laughs so hard that he has to lean over and press a hand to his belly. The old lady curses at the boy in disgust and tries to pull her dog away, but the German Shepherd just bends down to lick the little dog's urine. She shudders with horror, and the boy is rendered so hysterical that he is now rolling around on the ground, the last traces of winter's mud and dried leaves sticking to his back, spring's newborn hyacinths crushed beneath him. He tries to catch his breath now.

"Come back over here!" the man from the bench shouts, now in Polish, holding onto his head.

The beautiful, midday sun moves to a location central enough to sparkle as a reflection in the small pool behind them. The light diverts Anna's attention, and as she turns to look back at the scuffle she notices a lean figure in the distance, standing behind an old tree. His nose is thin and his eyes twinkle with the look of a small mole that has rediscovered his burrow. His white shirtsleeves are rolled up at the cuff and his hands are shoved into his pockets. Observing the odd couple, he smiles at the scene. He turns toward Anna and she looks back at him, but something about her attention makes the light fade from his face. He walks slowly to another tree, looking back at her every so often, and then away. It is as if he is being caught doing something wrong. What is it? She wants to understand. There is no way to know, as he quickly retreats behind a birch tree, branches twisted, like a mother's arms reaching for the sun.

XVI

There is a piece of music that runs through my heart whenever I need escape from the world. My piano teacher used to play it softly, and I would strain to listen to it from the cold hallway as I waited for my music lesson to begin. I could see that my teacher had been crying. She would carefully fold the sheet music and tuck it away beneath our lesson, putting a crease along the "t" in the composer's name, Satie.

The remains of my life are like this piece of music that mirrors all the last bittersweet traces in the world. They are: an image of Wolf, a lonely ghost-train ride. Only this melody knows how to make the pain of loss beautiful again. *Close my eyes and make me once more,* I ask. I ask again. I ask, and there is no answer. *Make me alive and whole so that he may come to me and our bodies can unite one more time. There is no love in the realm of ghosts.*

I tried my best to protect what was his, but in the end I could not win. His family may have moved on to the other side, but somehow I cannot. I am pinned to this earth, to rewitness my place, my life, even though I have none until I can love him once more or else find peace at last.

Are they waiting for me there? Really, I don't know.

He once held me against a tree in the oldest, most glorious forest in the world, where berries grow like flowers and leaves blanket the earth. It was there that we made love for the first and last time, where we created a new and secret life. No one will ever know. When he left, the baby died. Sometimes I blamed myself. Now I just reenter the dark, dark world, and whenever I think that I cannot take the pain anymore, that sweet, sweet music begins to play again. This is my music. The *Gymnopédies*. It reminds me of the sound of a man weeping, a beautiful woman lying naked in his arms.

XVII

Wolf feels the joy that comes with taking another breath. He is in Kraków now. He is alive. It is hard to know how he made it. The train ride was unimaginable.

It was almost as if an invisible source lifted him up from his place of pain, his position of subtle death, lying there on the ground of the town of N, an arm's length away from the house that had once sheltered him—the home of his family, his heart that ached with his first love. Who had bandaged his forehead? Helped him with his luggage, and brought him onto the train? *There are still kind people in this part of the world,* he thought, smiling between hallucinations on the train. Wolf could have sworn that there was a thin man with a mustache sitting across from him, every so often checking his bandage and his pulse. This man was very concerned about him, but whenever they arrived at a station and Wolf opened his eyes, the man was gone.

The scruffy little dog remains with him. From Białystok to Kraków that dog was nestled beside Wolf, emitting warmth as much as his little body could. Reaching into his bag (how was it that his bag had also made it onto the train?), he finds that he still has his daughter Leah's little piece of pink string. It is tied in a tender bow around his key ring. Relief washes over him. He has his bag. He has his life, his family in America, and all will be okay. He wants life. No more imaginings, no more dreams. He will find a place of burial in Kraków and recite a prayer, and then all those souls might begin to feel free. He is close to Auschwitz now, to the place where his family died, and here he will pray for them and put his sadness to rest. *No, I choose life,* he says to himself, only to go to sleep and dream again.

Every time Wolf closes his eyes he sees the same man, and then he dreams of Olga. The dreams come and go quickly. In the first dream, Olga is walking away from him in the forest. She is happy and free, collecting wildflowers in the summertime. He keeps calling out to her, asking her to turn around, but she never does. Finally he catches up to her. She leans her head against a tree and weeps.

In the second dream Olga is running through a house, screaming. Wolf tries to run after her, but soon he realizes that she is running from him. "But it's me," he pleads, crying with the pain of her fear, but she just keeps running. Finally she trips and falls on the stairs. All she can do is scream.

In the third dream, Wolf opens his eyes and sees the man on the train sitting across from him. The man smiles and holds out his hand. Wolf marvels at the strange absence of the man's hands—the sleeve cuff and the emptiness that seems to take form in an effort to move. How sheepishly the man looks down at it, as if to say that he too is amazed. This exchange of curiosity is long enough in the dream and it seems eternity is interrupted when Olga enters the train car. She slides open the door and looks down at the ground, her long gray skirt rustling against her military boots, loose strands of blond hair floating in the wind of her exhalation. The dog barks and Wolf shushes him. It was only when Olga sternly said, "*Cicho* (be quiet)," that the dog can listen. She sits across from Wolf on the bench beside the disappearing man. She looks at the man, and then at Wolf. She takes his hand.

The train pulls into Kraków Główny. Olga and the man are gone. There is such a feeling of emptiness to their absence, and yet Wolf reminds himself that of course it has only been a dream. But the feeling of comfort is still there. Wolf and the little dog disembark from the train with renewed strength. Passing a large window, Wolf could swear that he sees the man walking behind him, his face solemn, hands deep into his pockets, head turned to the ground. When Wolf decides to look behind him and finalize his imaginings—to believe or disbelieve—the image passes and his head just whirls.

XVIII

I could have taken that dog away from him if I'd wanted to, but I just couldn't bring myself to do it. He reminded me too much of my father, with the same dark hair and stooped shoulders, as if the weight of the world had been pushing down on him for a long while. You might say I don't look so much like him, but that doesn't matter to me. My mother had a Roman nose, blond hair and blue eyes, but my dad looked just like that. So did my sister. I try not to think about her.

It all started yesterday. I was standing at the railway station making my usual rounds. I had some French cigarettes I was trying to sell to make enough money to buy a loaf of bread and some seeds to feed the birds that have been hanging around. I hadn't even earned half of what I needed when this man came off the train and I nearly fell over because he looked so much like my father. Of course I knew it wasn't him, but seeing him stopped me dead in my tracks. I felt that whoever this man was— Italian or Jewish—I'd better pay attention to him. Not only that: he had an elegant suit made of some kind of material you don't see in Poland.

He had this funny little dog with him, and that dog looked so smart, and I cannot tell you how much I have been longing for something alive to love and hold. But this man was in a bad way. He had a bloody bandage on his forehead and a little leather bag, but it seemed like he could hardly carry the bag, he looked so weak. He had another man with him, a tall thin guy with a mustache who walked seriously, hands in his pockets. I couldn't tell if he was dead or alive (he had that funny smile the dead sometimes have). I am so used to seeing ghosts that I tried to just ignore him. Whoever doesn't talk to me, I don't talk to them. That's my way. It's better than walking around talking to people who aren't there. Makes others more at ease. People don't like it when you are too comfortable with the dead, and besides, I can't spend my time separating out the living anymore.

The man nearly passed out, he was so weak. I saw him leaning over a bench, dragging his bag on the floor. I ran over to him (even dropped a few of my French cigarettes on the floor, and left them there). The dog was whimpering at his feet. I asked him if I could help him, and at first he looked at me with fear. I thought he would faint, so I helped him sit down on the bench. I asked him what he was doing here, and he asked me who I was.

"I'm from here," I said. "What do you mean?" I added, tensing my fists and biting my tongue, as I have become accustomed to doing, and something changed in his eyes.

"Where are your parents?" he asked. "Oh, don't tell me. I know where they are." Then he mumbled something in Hebrew that sounded familiar, but which I couldn't understand. The only word that I knew was obvious. It was "HaShem."

Then he asked me in Yiddish if I liked potato pancakes. He didn't need an answer to know that I would say yes. He asked me to help him get to a hotel and take a rest, and then together we could get some lunch. I tried to cover the sound of my stomach growling.

He told me that his name was Wolf. He wanted to stay in the Jewish quarter, but I said better not to, and took him to one of the finest hotels in town. He told me he had money to spend. It was Monday and everyone was out on the streets soaking up the sunny spring day. Walking there was pretty tough, because the man wasn't feeling well, and so I had to carry his bag plus hold him up a little.

When we got to the hotel, I also had to hide the dog. The hotel is in a beautiful old building right near the center of town. I had always heard about it but had never been inside. They have a fine restaurant, big bathtubs, and faded carpets. Of course they didn't want to let us in. They didn't like the looks of me, and they didn't like the looks of the man either. First, he was wounded, and second, it was pretty obvious to them that he was a Jew. So he bribed them with some American dollars he had in his inside jacket pocket. I guess he'd put them aside for this kind of occasion. Now I knew for certain that he was a smart man.

They sent a bellboy in a red suit to take the man's bag and "escort us" to the room. Can you imagine? Just last week I was escorted out of the local police station, and here I was in the room of my dreams. I took the dog out of my coat and let him run free. The man said that he needed to rest, and suggested that maybe I would like to take a bath. I was happy to accept his offer.

Soaking in the bathtub filled with bubbles, I could not believe my luck. What kind of good fortune was the pill bestowing upon me now? Was I the luckiest kid in the world? I sang a few songs that I overheard last time I snuck into the cinema, and I washed my hair not once but four times. I used one of those special spray attachments that they have for the faucet, and I could have sworn that I was in heaven on earth. I stayed in that tub long enough to watch the water turn gray and my skin wrinkle up, to sing those songs more than once. Suddenly I was overcome with fear. I remembered that when I was little, this friend of mine got knocked in the head with a ball, and when he went to sleep that night he died. I wondered if the man had been snoring before, because now everything seemed so quiet. I jumped out of the tub, bubbles still on my skin. I ran out of the bathroom into the room, just to make sure he was still breathing. There I stood, naked and dripping soapy bubbles onto the carpeted floor. I strained to see if the man's chest was moving. After a moment, he lifted his head and opened his eyes.

"It's okay, child. I'm still alive," he smiled, and then laid his head back down. With eyes closed he smirked and said, "Now go back to your bath. Get clean so we can go fatten you up."

I was so embarrassed by my shrunken manhood that my face turned bright red, but I didn't really care. I was so relieved to find him still alive.

I dried off and dressed back into my oversize clothes, and when I emerged again the man seemed to be feeling much better. He had replaced the bandage on his forehead and was looking a lot brighter than before. I couldn't look him in the eye at first, but he told me I shouldn't be ashamed. Then the three of us—the man, the dog, and I—went out into the town, the other man suddenly tagging along again. I didn't say a word. Like I said, I have learned to ignore the presence of the dead.

Then something wonderful happened: The man took me to the same restaurant I had been to with the elegant lady. What incredible luck! I could hardly believe my eyes. We ate two portions of potato pancakes with sour cream, and then we had big bowls of borscht. I could see that the man was very happy as well. It had been a while since he'd had this kind of food, Polish style. Then we walked out into the street and the man took me to buy a new pair of shoes. Nobody was happier than I when I threw the old pair in the trash as we made our way to the park. And as he offered me an ice cream cone, with my choice of chocolate or strawberry, I knew for certain that this was the happiest day of my life.

XIX

Sometimes Anna thinks she sees Maryna walking toward her. As if the sunlight is gathering in an aura around one woman on the street, and that spotlight calls out to her, saying, "Look here, pay attention to me!" Anna raises her eyes and waves her hand, opens her mouth to say hello and greet an old friend. Lips part into faded silence at the realization that a stranger passes. *Remember this: the Jews are gone.*

"If we are ever separated will you look for me?" Rachelka used to ask, while playing games with Anna in the countryside. In that moment she would reach out her hand, fingers growing cold, palms sweating with anxiety. Anna would always assure her that they would never be parted. "You shouldn't worry so much," she would say.

"Just promise me," Rachelka would plead, a solemn look descending like thunder into those dark, misty eyes.

Sometimes an act so simple as peeling carrots will conjure up this memory, and Anna is wracked with a feeling she cannot explain. The memory of Rachelka's plea leads her back to an image of Maryna on a hot summer day, leaning out of the most glorious window in the building, her long hair blowing in the wind. The girls are happy because all of the governor-general's men are away. Maryna leans out the window, the Wisła River below, her face washed out by the sun. "If I fall, will you catch me?" she asks earnestly? Anna holds her breath.

When Anna was a small child and had just recovered from her illness, she was gifted a puppy as a reward for her renewed health. She felt so happy that she packed a knapsack with three apples, a lantern, and a book, and took the puppy for a long walk in the woods. They walked all afternoon until she was so tired that she cried. Luckily a hunter found her on his way home. Meanwhile, the dog had run away and was nowhere to be seen. When they finally found him, three days had passed, and he was lying sweetly in a heap of dry leaves just as if he had stopped to take a nap.

Whenever this memory arises, Anna still weeps like a child. It seems that nothing can make her cry sometimes, not the pain of losing all of her friends, not the loss of her home. But the memory of that little dog, so helpless and alone, and the feeling of responsibility that she had for his life, still tears at her heart.

XX

The day that Maryna was to be taken away, autumn had descended and there was a thick layer of dried leaves on the ground. The sky was blustery and gray, and the wind kept changing directions, stirring up the sad piles of leaves, carrying them from one corner of the courtyard to the other, as if there were somewhere to go. It was Friday. Monday morning the other Jewish housekeeper (whom everybody had thought was Polish until now) had been taken away. Maryna could sense that her time was coming. She was going to be exposed. The governor-general was out of town for the week, and the SS men were doing what they could to assert their power over him.

There were rumors in the ghetto about what it meant to be taken away, and about where one went from Plac Zgody, which served as Kraków's Umschlagplatz, never to be seen again. It was November 1942. The truth was becoming apparent, and the atmosphere was tense. Maryna received news that her mother had been taken away in a ghetto raid two weeks before.

The girls had spent the morning raking leaves and scrubbing the stone walkway outside. Fifty meters away some SS guards were joking around and smoking just as they always did, especially when the weather was sunny. In the afternoon, the girls were sent to clean the marble staircase in Niklas's building, an unusual chore for this time of day.

"You don't want us to clean his bedroom?" Maryna asked Pani Grzonka, the head housekeeper.

"Don't question me," Pani Grzonka snapped. It was not like her to act this way. They walked to the marble staircase, pails in hand, knowing that something was terribly wrong. Maryna took the second flight of stairs, and Anna started cleaning from the ground floor up.

Never before had Anna felt her own witchery so intensely. Never before had she felt so strong. *I won't let anything happen to her,* she told herself. *They will have to go through my body to get to her. Nothing can happen. I am a brick wall.* Her back was tense. Her leg muscles tightened. She felt like an animal ready to pounce. Anna looked up at Maryna, one flight of stairs above. Through the worn soles of her oxford shoes, through the short white socks, through the golden calves and the wrinkled seat of her starched uniform, through the tied strings of the white apron with the carefully embroidered lily of the valley, through the imagined white armband with the embroidered blue Jewish star pinned to the inside of her uniform pocket, hidden during the day but dreamt up at night, a steady stream of tears fell down Maryna's face and onto her dress. Her tears mingled with the soapy water, the salt from her heart forever embedding itself in the grains of the cold, smooth, white stone. Her hands trembled. As if someone had stabbed her back, she fell forward, exhaling deeply as if she wanted to howl, unable to catch her breath.

The front door slammed and Niklas came running up the stairs, his shirtsleeves rolled up at the cuff, his back soaked with sweat. He walked with accelerated determination and swept right past Anna, knocking over her bucket of water, spilling it all the way down into the foyer. Anna could see Maryna's face from her vantage point, could watch Maryna close her eyes and mouth something to herself. Through the courtyard window to the right Anna noticed several unfamiliar SS guards walking toward the building. The men stopped to have a smoke and speak with the guards stationed in the courtyard.

Anna was brought back to the staircase by the shout that escaped from Maryna's mouth as Niklas hissed at her to be quiet and then grabbed her by the arm. She could barely move her legs, and it was almost as if Niklas had lifted her into the air, her feet floating up toward the strange light cast by the blustery clouds pouring through the windows at the top of the stairs. The seat of her uniform was wet with urine.

Anna ran upstairs as fast as she could, nearly falling on the slippery stairs, wet rags still in her hands, as if she could erase the scene from reality. She tried to call out to Niklas, but something about the presence of those guards made her stop. Something within told her to be quiet. By the time she reached Niklas's room, he had taken Maryna inside and closed the door. Anna dared to turn the handle, but the door was locked, and from inside Niklas grunted at her to wait. She could hear Maryna sobbing endlessly, could hear Niklas whispering to her, but she couldn't distinguish his words. She wanted so desperately to hear what he was saying that she rested her ear against the door. She was too distracted by Maryna's cries. Then something very strange happened—Maryna spoke softly, peacefully. And then there was silence.

It seemed to Anna that the quiet was endless. Her heart was beating so fast that time felt both accelerated and slowed down, and there was no way to know just what was happening, how fast or how slow.

As if erupting from the wild beating of her heart, there was a sound that came from within the room of something opening abruptly—a door, perhaps? Then came a scream so brief that it was almost like a sigh, and then a loud thud followed by a chorus of horrible cries and punctuated shouts. The door to the room swung open and Niklas dragged Anna inside, throwing her down against the open bay window, ordering her to clean. His face was aflame and his eyes were swollen with tears. He flew over to the bathroom sink—the same one that had been the site of his first intimate moments with Maryna—and then he threw up into the sink. He wiped away the sweat and tears with a cloth placed on the basin, and then he told Anna to clean up that too. As he left the room, Anna imagined that she could see something. It was as if Maryna's white armband with the embroidered Jewish star was crumpled tightly in his hand. As he looked back at her with an expression that said, "clean or die," he quickly shoved the imaginary keepsake into his top dresser drawer. In a split second, he was out the door.

Anna's legs shook so violently that she thought they would buckle as she rose to peer out the open window. The sight of Maryna's body made her want to run to be sick, and yet she couldn't move. Maryna lay there on the cobblestone walkway, her arms and legs broken, her thick, chestnut hair splayed like wings, like a perfect fan around her head, blood flowing through the long strands of her hair like tiny riverbeds onto the walkway in a steady stream, drowning flowers still vibrant even in autumn.

Anna could see Niklas running out to address the crowd. There were the housekeepers, the SS guards, the yelping dogs, all of them gathered together to witness the body that was taken away from them too soon. She watched as Niklas demonstrated how Maryna fell out the window while cleaning the windows. How he tried to catch her, but it was too late. He pointed up at the window, at Anna looking out; he mimed Maryna's actions, Anna's too, shook his head, even laughed. He put on a perfect show. Then Anna watched as the SS men picked up Maryna's mangled body, threw her like driftwood into the back of their truck, and drove her away.

A pool of Maryna's blood was left on the pathway even after everyone had walked away. Anna imagined that through her spilled blood Maryna's life would somehow continue, seep into the cold stones, feed the ants and the worms and the plants, even the far-reaching trees stretching out toward the Wisła River, and day in, day out, summer, winter, rain or shine, it would move deep into the veins of those cold gray stones, forever changing their lifeless shade to her vibrant, most beautiful, crimson color, to remind the creator that there once was a wonderful being here.

*

There is a moment when falling feels like flying. An infinitesimal fraction of time freezes itself in the atmosphere, and at this moment you are the object of its fixation. So many thoughts flash through your mind in this instant. There are those you love, and you think of them. There is the sound of the world, the shaking, breathing, beating, rushing pulsing that you now realize mirrors the sound of your own life. Your heart is that beat, your blood is that water. And you would never ever be able to know this secret unless it came to you now, at the moment of your death. But you are rising up, and you have never been happier, because you know now that you are a part of this earth and beyond, that you breathe with this world. There are many beings, it is true, but there is also only one.

XXI

For two days after Maryna died, Anna's job was to scrub the cobblestone walkway, erasing any traces of Maryna's memory.

She couldn't stand working in the castle anymore. She was so alone and miserable, so sickened by the sight of any of the governor-general's men, that she would have rather died than remain there for another moment. Anna begged her father to help her find another secretarial job in town. It took him two months, but he finally found one, and she quit cleaning at Wawel immediately.

She did see Niklas again, but only once. The war had just ended, and the Russians entered Kraków. The atmosphere was jubilant, frantic, free. She was happier than ever because her family had been reunited, and because they were discussing possibilities for the future. She didn't want to think about the war or about the past.

Walking through Planty on a sunny spring day, one that was a lot like today, she turned to the left to look at some daffodils that were springing up when she saw the sole of a shoe sticking out from behind a bush. She was afraid to look, and still she had no choice but to walk around that bush and see what was behind. There lay what remained of Niklas, facing the sky, his face beaten, a dirty rope tied around his wrists and ankles, his ruddy cheeks drained of all their blood. She wondered what words had been exchanged, what altercation had made somebody want to kill him? Had he wanted to leave this world in the end? Had he shouted insults or begged for mercy?

While walking away from Niklas's dead body, Anna recalled the time she and Maryna had traveled with him to the countryside. The governor-general was out of town. It was the beginning of spring after a long winter. The flowers were budding and there was a newborn smell in the air. The atmosphere carried the headiness of love that everyone feels as winter dissipates. Even when there is war and you are lonely, even when inscribed in the wind is a secret dust that smells strangely sweet, and it is hidden and no one dares to speak of it, nothing can prevent you from wanting to make love when all of life is in bloom.

They were supposed to help Polish servants clean the basement of the governor-general's mansion half an hour from town. What Niklas really wanted was for Anna to work while he took a few hours alone with Maryna. Anna knew that everything existed on a precarious line, that the clouds could unfold, the earth swallow them up, her heart cease to beat, and all for what? She understood Maryna and Niklas in their craziness. They made their lives more vivid by making love to each other, so she kept to herself and did her work, just as she was told.

In the middle of the day Anna took her sandwich and went for a walk. She stumbled upon a herd of cows lying beside the road, soaking in the sun. They were spread out along fragrant patches of grass, red tags on their ears, demonstrating that they belonged to someone. Not far from the herd was a tiny group of four baby cows, huddled together. They looked especially cozy, but Anna's presence disturbed their peace, rousing the runt of the group immediately.

The youngest calf was so small that Anna imagined he could fit twice into the body of one of his brothers. He was a beautiful shade of brown, a color so rich that he seemed to be created not by a mother or a father but by the earth itself. He reminded Anna of Maryna somehow, which made her laugh as he ran around, parading his unique beauty. He came over to her and dropped his head, looking up with his big brown eyes and nuzzling her cheek as she bent down to touch his soft head. If she were a child she would have begged her mother to let her keep him. "Can I take him home, please?" she would have asked. But she wasn't a child anymore, so she caressed the head of that pure newborn calf and laughed and wept more than she ever could have before.

She continued to walk until she came across a field where a bicycle stood abandoned by a lone tree (she figured the person had gone over the bank on the right and into the stream), and there she found several cows grazing at three of the four corners of a plot of land. The clouds were so vast and majestic on that day, and she couldn't help but feel that if she could remain in that spot, everything would be possible. If she closed her eyes and inhaled the fresh air, then with just the power of her will she could erase the whole world.

Anna sat beneath the tree and leaned her head against the trunk, her hair latching onto the split bark at the base of the tree, as if it were hanging on to her. She watched clouds pass, felt them move through her, and she nearly fell asleep, so at peace was she on that day. But that kind of peace doesn't last long. She was surprised to see Niklas and Maryna come back for the bicycle. He was singing a German song and was happy, holding on to her long wet hair like he was Tarzan and her hair, the rope of freedom. She looked happy, too. Her smile was solemn and her eyes downcast, but Anna knew Maryna well enough to understand. Maryna touched her neck and belly with contentment. They were the only three in the world who would ever know the secret to Maryna's love.

As they walked back, the atmosphere was practically jubilant, and a couple of times Anna had to turn her head just to make sure she was not imagining things. She walked ahead of them, and more than once she heard Maryna squeal with delight. Niklas must have grabbed her breast or pinched her behind. They came back through the clearing where the cows were grazing, and the little brown calf came over to Anna, running along, playing and jumping. Anna didn't know why, but she could feel Niklas stiffen before it even happened. She heard Maryna gasp as she turned around just in time to watch Niklas grab the baby calf by the neck and drag him back the way they had come.

The calf did not cry out, and none of the herd seemed to notice or care. Maryna's eyes were filled with horror, and the girls ran after Niklas, Maryna ahead of Anna, breathing so heavily that she could barely run. They reached the banks and heard a painful squeal. Neither of them shouted. Only a tiny breath slipped from Maryna's lips. What had made them forget their place in this situation? Just moments before they had experienced an equality so real that they had been given the confidence to run for their lives, as if they could do something, prevent something, save someone.

XXII

At night I see the stars jumping to form a moving canopy above me.

Where are we going, my little feather? I wonder, but my feather just goes, no questions asked.

There is a lonesome lullaby that arises in this last passage of night. Sing to me, my little feather exclaims, breathing more softly than ever before.

XXIII

When it isn't the boy, it is Wolf who cries out in the night. There is an image that returns to him. It is a vision of Olga mounting a cold gray stone covered in moss and Hebrew lettering, her skirts slipping around her waist, a baby emerging in slow motion, falling through a ring of stars that have descended to Earth. The stars hover closely to the ground, keeping the baby suspended in the air, reversing gravity so the baby can float just above the ground. The decayed letters lift from the stones and mingle with the stars. Olga drops to the ground and the baby comes to life with a cry, rising up into the night sky. Wolf wakes up in a cold sweat. He opens his eyes. The stars are below him, scattered on the floor.

Wolf tells the boy the story of his life, about his love affair with a Polish woman and his marriage to his cousin, Chaja. He says that he felt like he was killing both of them when he left Olga and the town of N, but in America he grew slowly to love his wife, even more so when their children were born. With each new life, an old burden was lifted. He came to understand that commitment could be a more powerful force than passion—something that his rabbi had assured him of when he was uncertain about marrying Chaja and going to America.

Wolf says that when he found out the truth about his parents' fate, everything came rushing back to him. He could not stop thinking about Olga, about his mother and his father. Everything within him and beyond told him that he must go back home, if only to see. Nothing could have prepared Wolf for what he would feel. He knew, but he didn't really know until now that everyone he had known and loved was gone. His hometown, which was once more than fifty percent Jewish, was now a place inhabited by half a world, half a heart, and, most terribly, only half a soul.

XXIV

It is all a memory for me now, how I watch the stars gather to constellate me. One, two, three, they are coming, lifting me up into a new life.

"Pray for me," my little feather laughs, and I find one last way to play a melody.

XXV

I like hearing Wolf tell his life story, but I cannot tell him mine. I am too afraid that if I do, everything good will go away. I did talk a little bit about the old man in the camp, but not about the camp itself. I erased that memory forever, and I work hard to keep it that way. I see my life as split into two parts, one before the pill; the other, after. Before there was life and then there was the war, and anything after is another kind of existence. Survival and magic, that's how I like to explain what it's like now. Magic is the moon and its blessings, magic is the pill, the beautiful world, and now Wolf and his dog. They made me know what it feels like to hug again. I feel the dog's little heart beat next to mine. I have to admit that the first time it happened, I cried. I sat in the toilet and wept into a towel, so as not to worry Wolf. He was still very weak and in bed. When I cried, I could feel that there is a river inside of me so strong that if I cry just a little bit more, then it will never stop flowing. So I stopped.

I can't talk about what happened before. If I had a mother or a father or a sister or a brother I would talk, but they are gone, and I cannot speak of them at all. I don't want to call out their names or bring them any closer to me. I don't want to remind them of what they lost.

Wolf says he wants to go to Kazimierz to say a blessing for the dead. I tried to explain that the best place would be anywhere in Kraków, maybe on Kopiec Kosciuszki or beside the Wisła River. The land around Kraków is the closest thing he will find to a real family grave, but he feels certain about wanting to go to an actual Kirkut (cemetery). He is strict about which rules he must follow, and upset that there are so many he is unable to observe here. My father was that way, too.

This man is lucky that he has his new family in America, but here he is lost. He doesn't have the pill, like I do, to bring him luck and make the world around him beautiful again. But he does have me, and I can help him. He has the little dog, and the dead man who sits by his bed and waits. Maybe he is here to protect him, and so am I.

Wolf tells me that after he recites the prayer for the dead he will travel home to Brooklyn, USA. He says that he wants to leave this place forever. Now Wolf knows that New York is his home. He believes that after he recites the prayer, just like he tried to do in his hometown of N, then maybe his family will rest in peace. I tell him that he is right, that it will help, but I don't know if this is true. If Wolf could see all of those lingering spirits, like I do, then he would know that it isn't so easy to free the dead. They cling to the earth like animals grasping to their mother for milk. I shudder to think about it. When I remember having those feelings I begin to sink again, but thankfully I have the pill to lift me up from everything that wants to keep me down.

Maybe if I am lucky Wolf will bring me to America. Who knows? Anything is possible. Anything can happen. I believe that my pill makes dreams come true.

Tonight there will be a full moon. The sky will be beautiful and clear, and maybe there will even be a meteor shower. At least that's what the lady in the corner shop told me, and I would like to believe her, even though she is always swiping the last of my hand-rolled cigarettes.

XXVI

I dream about Rachelka. She is standing on top of the roof of our old school, singing a song she used to love. It is a Yiddish lullaby in which a mother sings to her crying child. It looks like Rachelka is singing it to the moon, but she is turned away from me, so it is difficult to tell. I am also standing on the roof, and when I look down at the school below, I see that the building is now made of nothing but a frame of fragile bones. Gone are the schoolroom floors, the ornate engraved walls, the beautiful paintings of surrounding landscapes. Only the old spiral staircase and a couple of rooms remain, one with a long row of single beds lined up against the wall.

The beams of the house shine in the bright moonlight, and when Rachelka sees me, she smiles. "Anna," she says, and walks toward me along the tightrope that connects her side of the roof to mine. She takes both of my hands in hers, and I notice that she is smaller now, or maybe I have grown, which is sad for me to realize, because we were once almost the same height. She points to the places where we used to live, and to the parks where we once played. She says that now all of them are gone. She gestures to the locked gate surrounding the schoolyard, and as I follow her hand, I see that outside the gate there are human figures writhing on the ground. They are moaning and crying, and when I look at her now, I feel afraid. But she holds my hand firmly and tells me to look one more time. She says that I can set them free. When I let go her hand I see that there is a ring of stars in the palm of my hand.

"Use it," she says, pointing to the gate again.

XXVII

There is a rhythm to everything, and sometimes souls must return to the earth. If your work was not done—but when is it ever done?—at least once, maybe four times, maybe even more, you begin again.

If I could stay suspended here, disembodied forever, I would. Then there would only be the dance of joy, the feather, the universe, my heart.

Part III

In the Beginning

I

Beneath the soot of this passageway there is a flower blooming in the dark. I saw it with my own eyes when we first came down to these tunnels. We marveled at the beauty of its petals and the strength of its thorns that pricked our fingers but never drew blood. In this tunnel darkness exceeds the depth of night. There is a texture to the pitch. As if once the sky existed without any stars, and that is where we stand now, waiting for the world to begin.

I walk in front of them. The footsteps of my men seem nonexistent, as they never make a sound, but they do rouse the dirt that has settled on the ground. Every inch of the tunnel is filled with sediment. The air is impenetrable at times, but we can still breathe, so we march on. One man asked if the footfall of a homeless man is heavier than that of someone who knows where he belongs. We all stop to think, but nobody knows the answer. Maybe it is even lighter, I say. Now there is nothing to hold us down.

"But we are going home, right?" demands Thomas, the thin young soldier, the one who is always crying out for his mother in the dark. "What about when we get there? Then we won't be lost anymore." I look back at the others. Nobody responds. We are coming to terms with the fact that we aren't going to find our way there anymore.

Now it is time to move through the dust and reach the end of the tunnel. We walk solemnly. Our conversation has come to a halt. Occasionally there is a grunt or a song. Thomas loves to sing German songs that were popular in Berlin before the war. His favorite song is "Lili Marleen." I used to feel sentimental when I heard that melody, like my heart was leaping from my chest into shattered halves remembering my sweetheart and my family, but now I just hear it and smile a little, like I am witnessing the last thread of my life, the final thing that will keep me tied to the world. Perhaps it is good that we are stuck in this tunnel, for in the next place there might not be any force of gravity to keep us down.

Now that we understand the truth about our lives, there is no longer any reason to cry. How did we discover everything packed into a tunnel underground? It is not as if there is a discarded match to be found or an old newspaper to tell us the truth about who won the war. But at some point we began to realize that we are among those who have died. Maybe it is the fact that these resistance tunnels seem to have no exit. Maybe it is because we noticed that our footfall no longer makes any sound. All at once our minds are coming together, recalling the quiet by the river, and that moment when a grenade exploded and time stopped for us. When winter lasted forever. Sometimes I wonder why that Polish man brought us down here. Did he know something we didn't? Did he wish us harm or did he wish us well? He knew who we were and the truth about what had happened, and yet he told us nothing.

II

When the dark is so deep I have moments in which I am afraid. Will leaving you, my feather, mean that one of us will disappear? Is it not our love for one another that keeps us suspended here so perfectly? Without me here, what will you do? Will you wait for me to return? When you see me again, many years from now, what if I am changed? How will you recognize me then? And if you don't know who I am, how will you find your way to love me once more?

III

I step on a mound of dirt, and another explosion of dust rains over us, extinguishing our last little light.

"What will we do now?" Matthias asks, cleaning his face with an old dust rag.

"How am I supposed to know?" I answer, annoyed by my position of power. Death has not made me a subordinate yet.

Thomas kneels on the ground, his head in his hands. "Oh mama," he moans. "I can't take it anymore. I want to die! I cannot stand it!" He grabs a knife from Matthias's belt, and with shaking hands, slits his own throat. Nothing happens. His suicide has no effect. He screams in horror, and though we hear his howl inside ourselves, on the outside world, in the caverns of this tunnel, it makes no sound. Hearing his cry feels like dying for the first time.

Thomas grabs onto Matthias's boots and tugs at them. Matthias, who is quick to anger, bends over to slap him. Thomas cowers and cries, and the sound of his terror penetrates us all. Matthias grabs the collar of Thomas's jacket and shakes him, as if he could rid him of his sadness by making him more afraid. Thomas holds the knife up in the air, his strained right hand fiercely gripping the ivory handle, now rocking and emitting an open-mouthed moan of lost desperation. We feel the reverberations inside our chests.

The anger drains from Matthias's face. "That's alright, kid," he says, gently now, pulling the knife from Thomas's taut hand. "That won't help you anymore." Matthias tucks the knife into his belt and kneels beside Thomas, who is now crying into the hollows of the earth, just like a child weeping into his pillow at night.

Matthias sighs. "We've got to keep on, Thomas. You'll see. Everything will be better soon." Thomas grabs onto Matthias's legs as if they are his last chance for salvation. Matthias gives in and cradles Thomas's lanky frame in his strong arms. He rocks him gently, petting his hair like a mother would her child, soothing him with all the kindness he can muster in the world.

How small is one tear? Not even a spider could bathe in its expanse, but his tears continue to pour forth and collect into a body of water, forming a miniature ocean that swells with the movement of his heart, a well that springs from him and moves upward, shifting airborne dust into a singular wall that separates my men from the end of the tunnel. His tears create an upward moving waterfall that rushes behind the wall of dust, casting raindrops of sediment in our direction. We are silent and amazed.

Thomas is the first to notice. A shiny button from his uniform deflects light onto his face. He looks up from the comfort of Matthias's lap and sees something shining in the distance. It is subtle at first, but then it grows stronger, emitting a humming sound loud enough for us to turn in its direction. The light filters through the layers of water and dust, creating a dim glow that shifts across our bodies, illuminating us to ourselves. We are no longer hidden in the dark as we step through a cascade of dust and water and into the light. I am first. I lead my men. The river of tears washes all the dirt and soot from my uniform and body, and I emerge in the mouth of a cave that opens onto the night sky.

This feels nothing like being on the earth below. It is as if we are up in the sky, floating on a cloud. Stranger is the sense that this was our reality all along. Something kept us ignorant. My men come out in awe, one by one. As babies we came into this world and proved our force of life with a wailing cry. Now we stand in silence and there is nothing concrete to separate us from the spheres all around. With just one step, the heavens rise to meet us.

We are at one with this metallic atmosphere, these rotating planets in the night sky, our bodies drifting toward a crescent moon.

IV

It is incredible to think that even after you have died you can still have the capacity to dream, but you can. It feels so different, like there is no separation between one moment and the next. You can choose to call one experience a dream, while the other, you don't. In the dream where the man sets me free, I return to the school completely changed. It is easy for me to reenter the building, and for a moment I wonder why I am doing so. Why don't I lay my sandy sheath down on the ground, or on top of a factory roof, stand naked beneath the moon, and let my blanket of sand give rise to a desert landscape? I could wander aimlessly for one thousand years, but it would make no difference. There isn't one Sarah that doesn't know the secrets of my heart.

In my dream I feel so free wandering the dark city at night. Naked and invisible beneath my shimmering shawl, I come to a group of men on the outskirts of the city. They are standing around a large metal garbage can where a fire is burning, drinking from amber bottles, talking excitedly. They have shaved heads and are wearing sport clothes. Some of them have black drawings painted onto their skin, just like the tribe leaders in Papua New Guinea. I notice their empty eyes, their wild smiles, and their brisk movements, and for some reason I remember the German soldiers who locked us up in the school and burnt us alive. I recall the sound of their voices and the sour smell of their breath that traveled with the shouts that sent our souls running. And oh how it felt when there was nowhere to go.

I watch them without being seen, but when I move closer, my shawl slips, and so does my invisibility. They spot me bending over to pick it up.

A warm breeze picks up fragments of dust in the night air, which sparkle as they pass over the fire. The man with the most drawings on his body, the one who seems to be the leader of the group, stands up and points at me, and the others nod in agreement. My heart races wildly as they kneel down in a circle, and the man gestures for me to come. I have no choice but to go. I pick up my desert blanket and walk over to them. They lay me down beside the fire and take turns marking my body with black ink and a pen that sizzles. I don't resist them. I give in to the initiation. They draw lines across my wrists and make a big double loop that twists around my belly button. They write Hebrew letters in a constellation pattern on my back. How do you know them? I ask, but they just point up. Then they write the words, *oved kochavim,* the servant of the stars. Even though I don't see the words, I know they are there. Now I understand that this phrase can have new meaning. These are letters I know by feeling. Together, they can recreate the world.

Each man writes something different. When they finish and change turns, the one who is done kisses me on the forehead, and allows the next man to come in. I have never made love. I never in my life had even the chance to kiss someone before I died. The way these men take care of my body, the way they mark it and release it, somehow makes me feel that they are helping to set my soul free, which is how I always imagined it would feel to make love.

When they are finished, they wrap my body back in the blanket of sand. They show me the way. I say goodbye to all of them, one by one, and with each farewell, I kiss them on the lips. I see how our tender exchange has changed them. Their gaze is no longer filled with hatred and emptiness. They tell me I have saved their lives.

I pass invisibly back through the streets of the town that I have known and loved. Now it is no longer a burnt-out wasteland. Everything has reversed to a time when the city was still happy and alive. I pass by families coming out of the theater, see businessmen laughing in local cafés. I even see my dear friend Anna walking down the street. She looks older and tired. She walks beside a very thin man with a mustache. They speak together in a quiet, serious manner. I call out to her, but there is no need. She doesn't hear me at all.

I pass by the storefront of what was once the best clothing store in town. All of the lights are turned off, and in the big glass window there is only the faint trace of a mannequin dressed for her wedding day, her young groom standing beside her in a gray suit. There are young fashionable mannequins, all standing at attention, looking out at the world, waiting to be chosen. I don't know how it happens, but I catch my reflection in the glass window. My body looks the same as it always has, artful, even, with all of the paintings that it carries. My hair, which was always black, is now long and silver, as if it has captured the light of all the stars.

When I arrive at the school gates, I pause before I reenter. The same man is still standing there, the one who let me out, ready to let me back in. It is as if he has been waiting for me there all along. He doesn't smile or wink this time, only solemnly opens the metal bars, which he closes as I enter, my shimmering sheath catching onto the latch of the gate, remaining there. I walk inside. I am in my school uniform again. As I climb the winding staircase toward little Sarah, who sits solemnly with her head in her hands, I wonder, how can it be that everything is different but nothing has changed? When little Sarah sees me, she smiles and touches my long gray hair.

V

It is easy to wait when you know that somebody you love is coming. I had thought we were close enough that not even death could sever our communication, but I must have been wrong. Wolf, I have called for you not once, but over and over. From the eastern border of Poland to the western tip, I have asked for you to hear me, begged for you to come. Waiting for you is worse than waiting for the messiah. At least he offers prayers for his people to speak.

Have you become my God? I thought better of myself.

Today I wandered the bridges that cross the Wisła River and even penetrated its depths, just to see what was there waiting. There I saw a girl, a beautiful Jewish girl. Her hair was long and intertwined with the reeds that extend for miles beyond her figure, fish feeding on plankton that grew at its tips. She wore no clothes, but showed me how she loves to dance, to lay her tawniness beneath the surface of the water so that it catches the sun at just the right moments. I asked her name.

"Uh oh," she mouthed, and swam away. A few minutes later she came back with a long stick, and in the sand she wrote out her name. Maryna. I smiled and told her it was a beautiful name. She showed me a small cache of things she kept to help entertain herself. There were old trinkets, like children's toys and colorful foil wrappers from candies discarded before the war. Memorabilia from happier times. There was even an SS hat, which alarmed me, especially when she tried it on and marched around as if she herself were a German soldier. I could not hide my disgust.

"What do you mean? How can you play that game?" I shouted in disbelief.

"Nobody can take away my fun," she told me, without even making a sound.

VI

These stones are perfect for paving roads. After all, you can't find any new material nowadays. Everybody agrees: you've got to be resourceful. Just because the war is over doesn't mean we have much.

So how to do it? You bring a rope, a wheelbarrow or something solid on wheels, and a knife or two just in case somebody decides to mess with you. Often the Germans already damaged the stones, or else we were forced to do so ourselves, so why not tow them off? Half the work has already been done. Nobody is coming back to visit them, especially not in eastern Poland, where so many mass murders took place.

Ah, but there are so many uses for these stones. They may be only made of granite, but sometimes you can still find a grave made of marble. You might even be able to remove the inscription and sell it off as a gravestone for a Pole. If not, you can always use the stones to build a new road. All you have to do is turn it over to hide the inscription, and nobody will ever know the difference. Look how easily you can make history disappear. We have a black market going among those of us who work in the cemeteries. Nobody is looking. Nobody can afford to waste anything useful nowadays. Nobody cares. Nobody will stop you. So maybe you do it at night, just so you don't show off. After all, somebody might get mad at you for disturbing the dead or for some other nonsense like that. Who knows? They might even get jealous about your taking some of the town's most valuable supplies without asking. But tell me, please, exactly whom would you like me to ask?

VII

Saturday evening as the sun goes down, Wolf puts on his jacket and removes the dressing from his forehead. He says a prayer. (How strange to do with no kippah, no tefillin, no tzitzit. Will HaShem ever forgive him?) He then takes his bag, the dog, and the boy and checks out of his hotel. There is a train leaving early the next morning that is headed west toward the countries that will lead him to the port, from where a boat will take him home.

And how does he define home now? A bed to rest his head where he knows that he is not taking anybody else's place? Familiar smells and sounds? A place that is filled with people he knows and loves? You can change a person's language. You can take from him everything material, and yet you must leave him something to love. And if there is no person left for him to love, then give him an idea that will keep his heart beating for just a few moments more.

And what about the boy? What will Wolf do with this miraculous boy? Who will care about him if he leaves him in Kraków alone? This is something he hasn't decided yet. He could leave him money, his address in America, what more? The boy does not have any papers. Perhaps he could take him home with him. What would Chaja say? Surely she would understand. And how would the whole family adapt? How would the boy respond to living in a home with rules after being on his own for so long? There are so many questions and yet there is no time to answer them, and so together they go.

Nights in Kraków are rarely like this. The cloud cover has retreated and the moon is so full that it is swelling with the luminosity of its own beauty. A rare occasion here. The occasional cloud does manage to pass over, and when it does, it creates a refraction of light, like a dim rainbow of the soul that curves around the circumference of the body of the moon, as if to say, now, this is love.

How lonely the moon must be, the boy thinks to himself, as he walks ahead of the group. He is so caught up in his imaginings that he does not notice the woman following them. Anna has just finished her shift selling *paczki*—doughnuts—at a little bakery on Ulica Krakówska, her Saturday job. She had thought about attending mass, but when she recognized the boy, the one whom she had recently seen in the center of town, she felt compelled to follow him. She has been haunted by his face and wants to know more about him, and also about the foreigner and the odd, thin man who walks beside them yet manages to look completely apart. Maybe it is the madness of experiencing so much loss in such a short period of time, but lately she believes in signs. Anna often thinks back to what happened in recent years and wonders why she couldn't have seen what was coming. How is it that she couldn't have known what was to be? She ignores the voice in her head that warns her not to go with them, and follows them down the street. Something inside tells her that she must.

Yes, the moon must live a lonely life, the boy repeats to himself, catching the glimpse of an ornate relief windowsill depicting an angel and a woman locked in an embrace. In the apartment beyond, an elderly couple count their money, discussing what food they will buy for the following week, and whether or not they can afford to eat meat. *At least the sun has its own phenomenal heat to keep the moon company,* the boy continues, passing by an empty building that was bustling with family life just a few years ago. A cold wind passes through the dark, empty doorway. The sun's rays touch down to earth, to the plants, to the water, to the skin of its people, transforming everything it dares to impact and even that which it doesn't. It affects people's lives. It is nature. It helps new life to grow. There is an exchange of energy to keep it going, but with the moon things are so different. People look at the moon, and feeling just how far away it really is, they suddenly feel very alone. They can sense its light and its glow but they can rarely feel it on their skin, even though they long to know its touch. They cannot get close to it, no matter how hard they try, and sometimes that is a painful feeling, wanting to be near something that is so far away. They watch the moon shrink and they watch it grow, but they will never know what it feels like to lay in its arms.

The moon is as powerful as the sun, but it works its magic in secret ways. Maybe that is why people say that the moon is feminine, because women are more mysterious than men. The moon has a magnetism that moves the waters in and out and up and down, and can do so inside a woman's body, or at least that is what I have heard, but I cannot always rely upon other people's stories to know the truth. Maybe I don't care anymore about what the truth has to tell me, anyway. Maybe that is why I love the pill so much, because it helps me to see the world how I want to see it, and if I want everything to be happy, then it is. Look how my optimism has brought me good fortune. Now I have Wolf in my life, and even a little animal to love and hold. I admit I am afraid of losing them. Wolf is leaving on the early morning train, and I wonder what will happen to me then? Will he take me with him? I want to ask him, but I can't. I am too afraid of what he will say. He has already given me everything. But oh how I long to stay with him. Even the pill will not heal this wound in my heart after he leaves.

Will it be too sad for Wolf to go into Kazimierz tonight? This I wonder, as we walk there in single file. I am used to the death and the graveyards, but for him it is all still new. This place isn't sad because it is a cemetery, no, of course not. It is always comforting to sit in the resting place of the dead. What is sad is the absence of names, of coffins that should be here, the secret presence of people who want to be buried, the ones who sleep in the rafters of the old factories, who swim the depths of the Wisła, who climb the roof of Wawel Castle trying to get closer to home. They are all stuck between worlds, just like the woman I saw wandering the tombs the other day, and just like Wiktor, our solemn guide, who means to protect and help Wolf, though I am not sure just how he can.

But somebody still loves us. This, I do believe. I don't know why, but I know that even while I sleep on the grass beneath the bridge I am never truly alone. There is always another day, always a pigeon to nestle in my arms, always a chance to begin again.

VIII

Last night I dreamt that the war had never happened and I was with my classmates on the outskirts of Łódź. We were playing hide and seek, and at a certain point I was the only one around. I decided to hike up a hill that was wet with mud. When I got midway, I stopped to take in the view. When I turned to continue walking, I saw someone lying on the ground. I moved toward the figure, and as I got closer, I realized that it was Rachelka lying there, face blue, scattered black hair exposed, eyes closed, body buried up to the neck in a mound of mud. I wanted to wake her with a kiss, but just as I neared the earth she disappeared, and all that was left was a pile of white feathers that fell gently to the ground and a small paper sign that read *Rachelka* in painted cursive letters. It was as if a bird had disappeared in the wake of my kiss.

IX

This cemetery was founded in 1800. It stands at the edge of Ulica Miodowa beside a stone overpass where elevated train tracks run diagonally alongside the grounds. Surrounded by a high wall made of brick and stone, it is not as beautiful as Remuh, but Remuh is no longer a working burial ground. Active for more than two hundred years, Remuh burial ground was shut down in 1799. There were also two other new Jewish cemeteries in Podgórze, across the river, but with the creation of Płaszow camp nearby, they were gradually destroyed. Remuh rests behind the tiny synagogue of the same name, and there you can find the tombstones of many important religious and historical figures, including the great Rabbi Moses Isserles, after whom the cemetery is named; Joel Sirkes; Rabbi Yom-Tov Lippman Heller; and many others who ask to be remembered. Remuh lies on tenderly sloping ground, the perfect resting place for those who have reserved a place for their memory. One cannot peer at Remuh without wanting to enter, but it has been locked now for many years. The only way to enter is through the courtyard of Remuh synagogue.

This cemetery where we stand at the end of Ulica Miodowa is still in use, though during the war, once the ghetto was built, it was closed for a time. The main pathway was destroyed, and so was the front. Many of the most beautiful graves were destroyed, especially those built of expensive material, such as marble, granite, and syenite. Those gravestones could be used to pave roads, or reused in other, new Christian cemeteries. Now that the war is over, there have been several instances of people taking gravestones, especially those valuable ones that remain, though this practice is more common in other regions of Poland.

X

There is something in the atmosphere tonight that makes Wolf pause at every corner.

It is almost as if I am dizzy, he thinks, perplexed by his disorientation. *Everything has happened so fast. What is most amazing is how the world can fall apart, and yet we are all alive, still standing, moving, breathing our air together as if we knew how to share. My heart, my limbs are cut off, and yet I walk down the street looking to the outside world as if nothing has changed, as if I am whole. One era ends, another begins.*

The little boy pauses at a stop sign to gaze up at the moon. Wolf notices his wiry frame, slight even for a boy of eleven. For the past five years this child has had hardly anything to eat. How can Wolf think to leave him behind? The muscles on the boy's arms are pronounced, and his sandy hair stands on end, as if it too is on the lookout for trouble. How will years of struggle and malnourishment take a toll on his growth? It is hard to know. Somehow Wolf feels protected by this child, and yet he wishes that he had the capacity to protect him more. He decides that he will have to take him back to New York with him, no matter what. He tells himself that no matter what they have to go through to make it happen, he is ready to suffer the consequences. He has no power to abandon another soul.

They arrive at the street that leads to the cemetery. It curves as if to create privacy and prevent outsiders from looking in. When the gates of the burial grounds come into view, Wolf is overcome by a wave of dizziness, and he finds it difficult to catch his breath.

"Maybe we shouldn't go inside," he says in a whispered tone, as if trying to convince himself, and grabs hold of the boy's arm. The boy stops. The dog stops. Wiktor stops. Everybody waits for Wolf to continue.

"But this is why you are here, to do this," the boy says, pleadingly.

"Yes, of course. You are right," Wolf says, taking a breath and shakily buttoning his jacket closed. His next step is firm. The group continues.

When they squeeze through an empty space between the cemetery's locked gates, they do not notice the three men struggling with a well-rooted gravestone in the right corner of the cemetery. They walk to the left.

"Maybe we should just smash the thing and sell it off in large pieces," one of the workers suggests, his slim pants clasped shut with an oversize safety pin, a smoldering hand-rolled cigarette permanently resting between clenched lips.

"No, we have to be more careful, otherwise there'll be no point," his overweight friend remarks, meticulously removing garden shovel after garden shovel of dirt from around the toppled headstone. "We'll ruin the grave and have nothing to show for it." The two men continue their hushed debate while their friend Paweł, an experienced stonemason ten years their senior, sits in silence on an old tombstone. He takes a swig from a small flask of vodka and leans back along the cool mausoleum to gaze up at the stars. As he lies down, a carefully engraved floral pattern winds around his head like a halo or a painted laurel wreath intended for the bust of an alabaster queen. It is hard to see everything through the newly sprouting branches of the big old trees, but much of the night sky is still visible, as it is still early spring. Little green shoots have no power to obfuscate the sky. Paweł pulls a toothpick from the deep grooves between his teeth and uses it as a baton to gesture at astrological configurations in the night sky. He cannot be bothered with his friends' debate. They are the ones who work here, who ripped a hole in the gate. They are the ones who need to figure this out. He was asked to come along as an extra pair of hands, as muscle, as backup, and nothing more, so he is happy to keep his mouth shut. He would rather focus on the outline of the big dipper anyway.

The gate is locked for the night, but the stonemason and his friends have left a gap large enough for a man to pass through. As for getting stones out, the men have a plan. Tonight the moon is so bright that every path is lit and there is no need for a lantern. It is the perfect night for doing this.

Wolf and the boy squeeze through the gates.

Anna stands breathless outside the cemetery gates, peering onto the scene. *What the hell am I standing here for, anyway?* she shouts internally, but for whatever reason, she is unable to move.

As they proceed toward the left side of the cemetery, Wolf and the boy are so focused on the task at hand that they are oblivious to the three men at work behind some trees on the right. They do not notice Anna standing behind them, breathless at the gates. Even the boy does not see Olga lying on the ground. She is doing her best to disappear into the earth, though she knows it is an impossible dream. Wiktor senses the presence of someone else like him, and moves off from the group to find this person. Olga lies there recalling an image of two swans floating along the Wisła River earlier today. Love and devotion are everywhere in nature, but she cannot keep anything for herself. When she sees the tall thin man standing above her, she does not blink an eye.

"I am ravaged," she says to him without even opening her mouth to make a sound.

"I know," he responds gently, bending down at her side, removing his hands from his pockets to demonstrate that he has none to show.

"I have nowhere left to go, and for some reason my spirit cannot move on," Olga says to the man. "I want to cry, but I cannot. I am empty."

"I know," he repeats, speaking in his Silesian dialect. He reaches down to scoop her up into his arms. "Come with me," he says. Olga rises to follow him, her long gray skirt rustling in the wind.

Wolf places his bag on the earth beside the newly erected grave of Róża Berger. She was fifty-six years old. She was killed in a pogrom in Kraków on August 11, 1945. People are coming back. People are coming home. Those Jews that remain in this town are working to find the bodies of their families and friends all around Poland, so that they can return them to Kraków and bury them where they belong. Wolf doesn't see them, but he hears them call. He removes his prayer book from the bag and strains to see the Hebrew letters in the moonlight. The little dog sniffs around the surrounding area, where there are plenty of hidden treasures beneath the old twisted vines, the moss that for more than a century has spread across these grounds, blanketing the earth with its love and devotion.

"Bone of my bones, flesh of my flesh." These are the words that come to him from the Torah as a way to begin. "I traveled back to Poland so that I could be close to you. I thought I would feel you here, but you are already so far away. We regret everything. We weep for you." Wolf looks up at the night sky as a great black bird flies overhead, the sound of its wings stirring the leaves on the trees. The bird rests on the upper branches of a tree. Wolf takes a deep breath and sighs, "Please look over those of us who remain." He begins to recite *"El Malei Rachamim,"* the prayer for the soul of the departed, with the quiet soulfulness of the brokenhearted. "God who is encompassed with mercy." With each word a weight is lifted from his chest. Soon he feels light. For a moment Wolf imagines he could leave this world behind, shirk his responsibilities and the unbearable pain of living with so much loss. But then how would he do justice to his life and to theirs? No, he must remain here, in Kazimierz, in Poland, in America, on the ground.

The dog lies down in the dirt and listens to the song of his new master, glassy blue eyes tilting toward the heavens. The boy steps off to the side, in the direction of an intact family grave, and sits down on the cold stone lip of a tomb. He feels shy about Wolf's words. Wolf has distance from the war in a way that he cannot. For Wolf there is a process of mourning and praying and remembering, but for him, there is only a way to live. He leans back against the cold stone tomb, unknowingly mimicking the posture of the man lying at the cemetery's opposite end.

Now the full moon is rising to a visible position in the sky. It is coming up over Kopiec Piłsudskiego and the abandoned buildings of Podgórze, where the sounds of the ghetto and of the Płaszow camp are still audible to some. The moon is turning its way around the stars, the stars are revolving around the moon, and our world circles around the sun. Everything is moving all the time, and yet if you look up and out, are you able to know and remember that you are on a rotating globe suspended in the atmosphere and that only gravity is holding you down?

This prayer is underway as Olga and Wiktor approach Wolf and the boy. When Olga hears Wolf's voice her eyes dart around madly, desperate to seek out the source of the sound. Wiktor carefully observes how her face transforms. When she sees Wolf, she jumps behind a tree. She has waited for too long, and doesn't know how to behave. Will Wolf see her there? Will he feel her presence at all?

At this moment a mouse runs beneath the vines twisted beside the stone walkway, and the dog jumps up to follow the mouse, barking excitedly. Wolf continues his prayer, only louder now, and the chaos of sound reaches the front gate, where Anna is standing. The cacophony floods the cemetery, extending to its four corners, including the place where the men are busy debating the best method of removing a headstone. Paweł, the lazy stonemason who is resting against a tomb, flask in one hand, cigarette in the other, jumps in attention at the noise coming from the other side of the grounds.

"Did you hear that?" he asks his buddies, but they pay him no mind. He asks again.

"Must be from the street," the thin one says.

"Maybe it's a ghost," the other man laughs.

The barking continues, and so does the prayer in song. Filtered through the branches of the trees at the center of the cemetery, the sounds become distant and formless. Paweł listens carefully, jumping to his feet.

"No, it is something," Paweł insists, reaching for a rock from beside the grave. Sweating now, he edges toward the sound. There is an unexplainable anxiety pumping through his blood. He is unable to distinguish fear from anger, unsure what he is anticipating, if it is just some kind of ghostly presence or else another man, a stonemason, maybe, trying to beat them to the best gravestones around. Determined not to let them win or hurt him, whoever they are, he walks through the trees, approaching the source of the sound, a large rock in hand. Startled by the sudden rush of wings as a black bird flies overhead, he ducks down, nearly falling back into a freshly dug grave. He has to scramble to retain his balance. His head reels from the rush of alcohol and adrenaline. Now his heart is in his throat and he is in a rage as he approaches the figure in the shadows. This area is dark, but he can make out the silhouettes of two men. One man is standing, the other is sitting down. There is also a small animal on the ground.

Wiktor is waiting amid scattered trees. He resembles the stark branch of a tree that has yet to develop new leaves. He is lost in the moment.

Olga is swooning in the moonlight against a tree trunk.

Anna is standing at the gates, tiny beads of sweat pouring down her face as she sees a man crossing the cemetery toward Wolf and the boy. Screaming on the inside, she is suddenly frozen and unable to act.

Just as he did after the train hit him, Wiktor's body rises and sweeps now through the branches and the tombs, aboard the faint breeze of spring. "Wait for me!" he would shout if only he could. "Don't move." But there is no longer any possibility for sound. The best he can do is to rustle the branches of a tree and make a leaf fly into the approaching man's face, but his diversions are useless, and they come too late.

XI

A man's face is painted on the side of a building right here, on this abandoned street corner. His face spans the entire brick wall, but you cannot see him unless you come here at night, close your eyes to the world, and ask for his face to appear. Then you will see the white lines of his eyes, the charcoal outline of his lips, and the great white feathers that span from his head.

This painting will smile at you when you ask it to, you will see, but for now it is no more than a secret mirage. It will be here one day, out for everyone to see, many years from now when this story is well hidden and everyone can celebrate in Poland freely and there will be songs danced in the streets of Kazimierz. You might not believe it now, but you will see. The man's face will reign over this district of forgotten souls. You cannot imagine it, can you? But someday it will happen. And the sight of such change will make you want to weep.

XII

Pain is so very strange. When it comes suddenly, sometimes it can get lost in time and you feel almost nothing at all. First there is a shock and everything moves slowly, and then the world is still, everything has stopped. Then you are floating, about to separate from your body, until the pain brings you back, and you are abruptly reunited with yourself. And then you pray for escape, because it is almost too much to bear.

I didn't see him coming. I was listening to the sound of Wolf's voice as his prayer rose into the heavens. The beauty of the prayer for the dead, which I hummed softly to myself, was enough to make me want to cry. I could reach that well inside that I have been trying to hide and let the waters of my heart flow until I drown in their depths. It is possible, you know. The body contains so much water that if you let your sadness free it can drown you in an instant. When I leaned back against the cold tombstone I was certain that this would happen to me, *yes and now,* I said to myself, looking up at the moon, so swollen and beautiful that I could almost feel it pulling at my heart. But the dog's barking distracted me, which was good, because then I knew for sure that this would not be my day to cry or to drown.

Wolf stopped praying and bent over to see what was happening with the dog when I heard a thump. The sound came before the slowing of time and also before the pain, as if my heart had skipped a beat and I could not keep track of what was real. It went like this: first a loud thud, then a cold feeling on my face, then Wolf shouting and the dog barking. "Hush, please, could you just be a little bit quieter?" I wanted to whisper, but I was unable to speak. Then I realized that the ringing in my ears was louder than anything. What is that buzz inside my head? What is that well rising in my throat? Could it be that the dam of sadness has broken open at last? No, it was vomit and blood. There was a strange taste, and then a feeling that something was pulling hard on my head. And then came the pain. I tried to open my eyes, but I could not see. I felt Wolf's head and arms around me and his body trembling hard against mine. "Don't shake so much, dear Wolf," I wanted to tell him soothingly, but it was impossible at that moment to say those words. And then I heard the sound of many voices, like a chorus of men, women, and dogs, and of all the people in this world and beyond who wanted to save me but who could do nothing.

And now something incredible is happening. It is like nothing that the pill has ever given me before, like none of my prayers that have ever been answered or not been answered. If I could sing and jump with happiness, I would. First I depart from the tombstone up through the trees, so tender at this moment of spring. They bow gently as I pass, a black bird nodding its beak in my direction, as if to say, go on, it's your turn to fly. I am blanketed in the cold night air, the stars suspended around my body, just as if I were one of them. I lift up further and further, rising to meet the moon, and though nothing on the surface of the moon has changed, I can feel its delight at seeing me approach. I open my arms to welcome it just as it is welcoming me. You have never experienced such a warm feeling. It is the most beautiful thing I have ever known, like many temperatures of light and color passing through your whole being. Only you don't have a body anymore, so there is nothing to keep you from feeling that your being extends past the sky, past the world, even the universe. Your body becomes everything at once. More than holding that little sweet dog in my arms, more than how it felt when I was a child and my mother hugged me tight, before there was war and everything became night.

I see the moon smiling at me now, calling my name with my mother's voice. Is that her calling? Has she been secretly waiting for me all this time? Oh, Mama, you always knew just what I needed. You always did have a trick up your sleeve. I am going up to meet you now. And, Mama, I did what you asked. I never let myself be afraid. Can I cry now? Can I let my river of sadness run free? I don't have to. I am almost home. I look down at the cemetery and I see Wolf sobbing over my dead body. "Don't cry, Wolf!" I want to shout down into the blackness of the night. There I am, the shell of a human being, so empty without my soul, like a statue or a doll. I am surprised to see just how small I look lying there on the ground. For a moment I think to go back and help him, but I cannot. I am on to something else now.

XIII

Everything happens so fast, and from a distance there is only the racing heart and the night air to contend with. Anna doesn't see Wolf leap to save the boy, sitting beside him trying to stop the bleeding of his skull, yelling at the man with the rock to tie a tourniquet around his head. Most strange is that the man does exactly what Wolf tells him to do. When he realizes just what he has done, he becomes prepared to stone himself next.

No, Anna does not witness the frightening scene of the little boy losing consciousness, of Wolf weeping, or of the dog barking frantically, running around them in wild, near-blind circles, the souls of Wiktor and Olga shrieking at the edges, the violent man shouting and crying, "What have I done?! What have I done?!" as his friends run to the scene to fight with Wolf. She does not watch the man step in to protect Wolf from them. She does not see the thieves tell him that they had all better run, nor does she hear him respond by telling them to go to hell. Anna only sees the two men abandon their equipment and scurry out of the opening between the locked cemetery gates. As the second man, the thin one with the loose trousers, passes through the gates, out of the cemetery, she notices that he has a bloodstained handprint on his shirt. The red smear seems to stand on its own, lifted from the shirt in relief, vibrating in the strange half-light of night, blood pulsating in the street.

Now as she leans against the outer surface of the cemetery wall hoping for invisibility, Anna feels a hot wet stream of urine slide between her thighs. Nothing in this world, not even the sight of her friend Maryna's dead body smashed against the pavement, has ever been as shocking as the blood-stained handprint on this man's sleeve. She cannot shiver the image out of her mind. When the men are gone, Anna begins to shout for help. She rattles the gate and screams with everything she has. As if she could make up for everything she has lost, for everyone who has died.

An old man in his dressing gown comes running from a nearby building, and together he and Anna worm their way through the locked gates. There is such a commotion at the sight of the boy lying there in a pool of blood. Paweł, the drunk Polish man, lifts the boy up into his arms, as if he were light as a feather, and together the group, which includes the little dog and the sad foreigner, walk slowly out of the cemetery gates, Wiktor and Olga hovering above the scene in the branches of an unwavering tree.

XIV

The officer looks at me with an unfeeling expression. "Why are you here making trouble?" He asks. "Where are you from?" I pull out my documents and tell him I am about to get on a train out of Poland, and he stops his line of questioning.

I leave the child's body there, with the policemen and the drunken stranger who is now weeping with his head in his trembling hands, a long strand of cigarette ash falling from his fingers to the floor. I leave a part of me there, too.

I walk to the train station with the young lady who helped us at the cemetery, both of us weeping all the way. A young couple passes us and laughs. The woman asks the man what is wrong with us, and he calls us drunkards and they continue on their way. When we arrive at the near-empty station everything feels bleak, and for a second I wonder if there will be no train, but there it is, lights facing west. I board with the dog. She hugs me tight, trembling in my arms, skirt stained with fear.

My little dog stays faithful to me. He sits on my lap and looks out the window at the passing scene. The night is still shrouded in darkness, but I can see on the horizon that dawn is breaking. There is a thin pink line, a scar separating sky from earth, stealing the night away. When I close my eyes I see the train lifting up into the night sky, a shower of scattered letters falling like stars all around me. I could never gather them quickly enough. I can see Olga floating up beside me, her arms around the body of a small child. Maybe their souls are together now. I wonder this as I fall asleep. I don't know why I thought that I could come back and see. There is no home for us here anymore. Everyone I love, everything I touch. . . .

XV

There is a wind of energy inside every man and in everything, and I can see it now, though I never could before. You lay there sleeping, head loping against the windowpane, breath quickened, eyelids shifting with the movement of your dreams. My darling, Wolf, where are you flying to now? You were always distracted by your thoughts. Now I am one of them, sending you a question, hoping that you might hear my voice from somewhere deep within. I watch the open planes of your sleeping face as they twitch with questions and cries, insuppressible, also in sleep. I watch the movement of your breath as it runs through your skin and veins and even through your cells, pulsing your life through to the next vibrant breath. People are more alive than they can ever know. And though I have no chance to lie in your arms anymore, at least I am with you now. When you boarded the train I followed you, and now I am at peace. Without a body, but still on the peripheries, unable to quit the witnessing of this world, I feel safe now because I am with you, just as we are supposed to be. We are together again.

XVI

From above, this world looks like a sea of grounded stars or a light box with secrets obvious and exposed. On earth everything feels so complicated and unknown, but up here it isn't the same. You all linger there like you could make a difference, always saying, maybe this time. . . .

Part IV
The Feather

I

Death is all around, and it is impossible to sleep. Anna's heart beats so feverishly that it translates into a staccato rhythm in her dreams. In these visions, Maryna cries out for help. So do Rachelka and the boy. His skin is soaked in blood, his hair, matted. Red is everywhere. Red is the color of the rhythm that makes her want to run.

"Where were you?" Rachelka cries, spitting at Anna's feet. Her hair is gray, her eyes aflame with anger. She runs barefoot and wild into the courtyard and out into the street. Anna hears a scream so deep and enduring that it is impossible to discern where it is coming from.

Now she awakes with a start, and the first thing that she sees is Wiktor sitting at the foot of her bed. Wojtuś, who is not so little anymore, snores peacefully at her side. Anna sits up and jumps back against the headboard. They sit staring at one another for what seems like a long while. She marvels at the soft fuzziness of his kind face. Daylight is coming, and his image is fading with the increasing light. *Do ghosts disappear in the day?* She asks him in her thoughts. He takes her hand. She looks down to see that he has no hands but only colorless swirls of energy where hands and fingers should be. There is a powerful surge to their touch. He opens her palm, and in it he places a ring of stars.

"Set them free," he tells her, and she opens her eyes.

II

At the top of this wall leading to the churchyard there is a row of columns on which sit a group of saints. On the left stands a statue of St. Thérèse, and there is one of St. Anthony on the right. They are frozen in time, forever gesturing toward the sky. What are they questioning? One thing is for certain: there are truths to behold. During the day they subtly implore passersby to stop and remember them, maybe even go inside the church (light a candle, confess, attend mass), but at night these statues look like gods painted against the brilliant nocturnal sky. Above them hovers a scattering of clouds. On earth these statues mimic the central point of a cosmological system. We passersby orbit them in awe. We see how their flesh is made of stone, quivering at the subtlest level. Their life force is much more refined than that of a leaf, a tree, or even a blade of grass. Theirs is hidden somewhere far beneath. Look again and you will see. Their hearts are on their sleeves.

Tonight there is a black bird crouching on the head of St. Thérèse. This is no ordinary pigeon or crow, but a bird whose wings expand more than ten feet wide, a kind of bird you have never seen before. This bird has witnessed the construction of St. Mary's Church, has seen Kraków way back when. This bird watched over droves of people as they were shuffled like cards and ushered out of Kraków, then turned into dust. This bird has seen it all. And tonight it followed the wind to rest here for a while, gathering strength before its next flight. This bird has sat on the Temple Mount and listened to every song, every call to prayer. This bird knows every language and every psalm. Now Polish is the language that it listens to most. This bird has flown to America, where they speak with a dull twang. In a time of uncharted waters, this bird followed as one culture was destroyed, another swiftly born. Erasing the past has never benefitted any group of pioneers more. This bird has heard the pitter-patter of immigrant feet in a country built by foreigners for people who belong. America, where everyone is a stranger, everybody looking for a home.

This bird has seen great works of art painted and performed, has sat on the shoulders of Tolstoy and Tsvetaeva, of Debussy and Górecki, and on the windowsill of Kafka, where laughter and gloom always coexisted. This bird has listened to Mozart conduct his *Marriage of Figaro* at the opera house in Vienna, sat with the young composer while he quietly sang himself into his dying breath. "But who is that soprano?" he asked, a quiet murmur that came too late.

This bird has swooped over the tree where Buddha sat, carried an olive leaf to Christ as he wandered in the desert, laying it down by his side while he slept, eyes like the deepest muddy river, sun sparkling off its shallow surface. This bird has bathed his charcoal-dusted wings in the Nile, traveled the cosmos and beyond with her people in ancient times. He has dipped his longest feather in the dust of a tomb painted with Egyptian history, real, imagined, and forgotten, the tomb that was submerged in water and then projected into the stars. He then gave the feather to Maat, and now Maat weighs it against every heart. What heart is equal to the weight of a feather? You might ask. The right one.

This bird always recognizes the heart that longs to belong. The longing heart yearns for love, and this bird takes special care to watch over it, not because it is any better than the others, and not because the bird can do anything to alter its reality in the physical world, but because these hearts need more reassurance than others in order to feel that they belong. And when they are reassured by the quiet voice within, the one that is signaled from elsewhere, held still by the flapping of this bird's expansive black wings, then there is a chance for peace. And when this heart is at peace it can really love, and its love helps to heal the world.

III

Plaster my heart with silver and gold. Make the moon grow so big we can step on a ladder to greet it. These are the kinds of wishes whispered by Elżbieta's son, Wiktor's grandchild, little Mateusz, when he was just an altar boy. And when Mateusz was in trouble, he would turn his back on the family and stare at the wall. He could hold this pose with pride for hours until his parents had to beg him to turn around. What had begun as his punishment turned into a game in which he punished them. You could see early on that he knew how to win. What made him dream that he could leave this little town and become someone? As a teenager he stood at the summit of Rybnik, coal smoke burning in the dusk, shouting at the top of his lungs, "I will never leave this town!" But he would, and he would go far.

Days were spent playing soccer and hockey, running in the fields and through the forest where just a few years before Nazis had fought, where you could still find shells and bullets and other treasures left over from the war. Now there was a Gypsy camp in the woods, slightly removed from the riverbank, and Mateusz and his friends would gaze at the caravans from the other side, sneaking behind trees in the night, wondering what it was like to be on the other side. There was always a beautiful woman to watch and dream of as she bathed in the cool clean waters, unraveling her long black hair, which would float along the surface of the water, just like a mermaid's, as if no other woman had ever existed.

From this point on there would be only one female ideal in Mateusz's mind, that of a woman with dark and exotic looks. Yes, he would find his way to love Polish beauties with their long blue eyes and blond hair tied into a thick braid to match that of a horse's mane, but he would always dream of a dark woman until he found himself the right one.

What made Mateusz, a child of this old world, altar boy and rebellious one, shorts appropriately cropped for the times, young muscles strengthening as he grew into a handsome young man—a perfect mix of mother and father, of the dark looks and the gentle eyes—think that he could become an actor and leave this town? Was it that the black bird was watching over him? Burrowing close to his tender heart? Was it hubris? Was it a dream? Nothing that pulled at his heart and made him want to remain in the tender, sad world in which he had spent his entire life thus far could keep him from reaching for some bigger dream. Some unknown particle felt both within and without propelled him forward to Warsaw, into that drama school, text from *The Little Prince* in hand, sweating palms bleeding through the letters, dampening the page. But that didn't matter now. He knew the words, the right ones. The reading was from a section about a fox and the prince, about how loving someone imprints them forever on your experience of the world. You may know this story. You may have read it, too. And if you haven't, you must go and read it now.

IV

The first thing Wolf did, after praying, was to go to sleep. I lay my body down on top of his, as I would have done as his lover, as I have always wanted to do. I still remember that unbearable need to merge my body with his. People say that love is joyful. Why? I remember when we made love, I wanted only to cry. The joy of feeling an extension of his life inside of me was too much, because no matter what we did, he could never be close enough. Ecstasy lies right on the border of loss. I could not bear to love him, and yet I had no choice.

The boat rocks us back and forth as we cross the ocean. Sometimes the movement is gentle, like lying in a hammock or being cradled in your mother's arms, but at other times it is wildly violent, and Wolf lies sick in bed, moaning as he vomits out whatever food he has managed to get down.

We boarded in Hamburg.

I wonder how many lost souls have left Europe for other shores? I suspect that most of them stayed behind. When we first came aboard the boat, I felt so unsure. Where was I to fit in this tiny room with only a bed and a place for the little dog to sleep?

We are traveling to America now. I wander the deck at night and listen to people. Most of them have never been there before. A new life begins for us all. We look out at the uncertain world. I understand these travelers well. Our old world is lost in the mist. Wolf keeps mostly to himself. He sits in his room and reads a lot. Sometimes he stares out the small circular window in his room and watches the sea pass by. He loves to snuggle and pet the dog, whose old stomach seems to be stronger than the rest.

V

This city was destroyed during the war, but slowly things have been built up again. Some places have been renovated to look as if they were never even gone. There is a second coming, a revitalization of life, never to replicate what it once was, but now the city can be something else. When thirty years have passed, this city will become a monument to the socialist system. There are wide boulevards. There are statues bound together with pride in tribute to the worker, and there are also monuments to the past. Here uprisings challenged a reign of terror and despair. Ghetto Uprising, Warsaw Uprising, walls crumbling down, a cacophony of screams at dawn but nobody hears your sound above his own, basements filled with mothers and children weeping in anticipation of an uncertain end. That was Warsaw then.

Now thirty years have passed and everything has changed. Before World War II people called Warsaw the Paris of Eastern Europe. It is now Paris without the glamour, Paris without the fine cuisine, the outdoor cafés, the Arc de Triomphe, and the city lights.

It is here that Mateusz comes to study theater, and his world begins to open.

There is magic to standing in a black box with everything on the outside submerged in darkness, bright lights shining down on an imaginary world. You are the center of that world. Your breath reverberates throughout the darkness and people are watching and waiting to return your breath with a wave of intensity so honed that it might feel like love. There is an unexplainable transmission of energy in this dark house where every story is possible. Fake tears and blood are never really fake. Didn't you know? If you do this, if you give yourself over to the magic, then you can feel your body expanding to incorporate everyone, and you can experience the most wonderful sensation of oneness and you will feel that the whole world is in love with you, and you will shine like the brightest sun. There is a practice to living so many lives, but is there also a price? How does the individual survive when it spends so much time stepping into other souls? Who's to know? Maybe the answer comes later. Right now, under those hot lights, with the hushed silence of an audience at your feet, the consequences are nothing but an irrelevant dream. And the universe is rotating, and you want to bask in its glory, and you are calling out to the cosmos from the earth, and now, for just this moment in time, you are at home in this one room, and it feels like you are the central point of everything.

VI

The wings of a bird are not so different from the wings of an angel. And what about the wings of the mind? Remember you, the child? You also had wings. You lay beneath the clouds and projected yourself into their midst.

Freed from his obligations toward Wolf, toward Anna, toward the people of this world, Wiktor recognizes that the time has come for him to move on. But how does one go to the next level? Does it involve ascending or descending? Perhaps simply moving to the side? Leaving behind this world is something new, something he has never done before. He walks for hours toward the outskirts of Kraków, where there is a big stone quarry with pale blue waters the color of the brightest sky or the clearest mind. He walks down the rocky steps and looks up at the pink dawn. The water reflects this blush of life. And the mirrored beauty causes a surge of emotion in his heart that he has not felt since he died.

"But oh I will miss this world," Wiktor says aloud, to no one in particular, arms cast straight up into the air, chest heaving, weeping like he didn't know he could.

For a moment it seems as if he will be sucked into the earth. There is no freedom in hanging on to the familiar. A flock of birds flies overhead. Everything changes once again.

Now it is time for Wiktor to be set free, his old clothes disintegrating with each passing moment, just as the sky brightens incrementally. He steps into the waters, tenuously at first, but there is no shallow bank on which he can lean, so he must submerge himself completely. How is it to swim when you are no longer alive? There is nothing so beautiful. You can breathe water just as you once could the air. Everything is available to you as it never was before. You may witness a realm of microscopic creatures, for every molecule of water and life is moving together and there is no separation from one element to the next. I breathe, you breathe, as if there is someone to talk to.

Now Wiktor swims to the rough surface at the bottom of the quarry where there is a circular hole just big enough to fit his body. He swims down into the opening, which appears to be a secondary reflection of that ecstatic pink sky. As he moves through, a cold wind blows past his face, sweeping something away. He arrives in the garden of his childhood home, where there is an apple orchard and chickens run wild. There is that old smell of dawn coming over the fields and a sense of longing so strong that he must run, just as he always did, across the fields, away from home. Running wild, arms outstretched, hands brushing the tall prickling grass until breathlessness forces him to succumb. This is an image of his world, formed in childhood. This is the fullness of being alive. This time of his life has come to him once again. Was this feeling the cause of that strange, sad pain? *I can live it again, now, and everything is okay.* He hears his mother's voice calling his name, and when he turns his head to reply, the familiar world falls away.

You could call this darkness, only that everything is filled with light. The new world appears like the night, for there is a thick terrain of stars that is spread out in a twisted expanse before him. This is the whirling double helix of life, and also something beyond. This has no name. In the arms of the universe, there is nothing to see or hear, nothing to know. Gravity is a memory. I wouldn't dwell on it for long. The afterlife is weightlessness. One, two, three, go. Count your way to forgetting. Who are you now? You are the body that created the shadow. You are the sound that created the world. You shiver with the joy of being home again.

VII

Anna cannot go back to sleep as night changes hands with the dawn. First a line appears across the horizon like a pale purple finger reaching out to provoke the light. Periwinkle blue is met by a variation on pink so vibrant that it is always remarkable to see again. Pale crooked fingers spread further and brighten until the sky is all aglow and pink and purple, as if nature were blushing at her own ability. And when the atmosphere is cast in this particular shade of purple-pink, the light also tints the rooftops and the waters with its unbelievable expression of love. It is enough to make you forget the pain of yesterday and want to begin again.

The pink sky is aglow above the rooftops of Kraków and the looming church tower nearby. Even with everything that has happened in this city in recent years, it still looks storybook perfect at any hour. In the fog, in the snow, in the delicate smoke-laden wind of winter's reprieve, Kraków is always magical. Anna listens to the ticking of the old silver wind-up clock beside her bed. On a little cot across the room, her brother, Wojtuś, sleeps so peacefully, as if nothing bad could ever happen to him. Even now. Anna feels her soul wrestling with everything. Stars in my hand, what does that mean? She looks down at her empty palm and a sudden association comes to mind: the pattern on the ceiling of the old school library, tiny white orbs of light cast against a blue background. The mural was painted at the end of the nineteenth century. The girls used to love to play games of hide and seek in the library and to read together, sometimes adventure stories, other times romantic histories about knights or princesses. Aside from the schoolyard and the roof of the school building, which was always off limits but still used for games, the library was their favorite place for escape. And then there was a leak in the roof, and a mother crow made a nest for her babies hidden in the soft beams of wood. Eventually the ceiling had to be replastered, the walls painted over, and the family of birds relocated. Now the orbs of light were gone, and there was only a gray wall to look up to. But the magic of the past was never forgotten. The next autumn the Nazi invasion began, and Anna and her family left town. And soon after the school was burnt to the ground with the girls inside.

It is no longer possible for Anna to stay in Kraków and do nothing. She will return to Łódź, put a candle on those grounds. It is a small gesture, but it could help somehow. As if those girls are listening. *Most people wait for All Saints' Day, but I will go now,* Anna decides as she rises from her bed and changes from her old nightgown into her only dress. She puts on her stockings and combs her hair. She walks to the mirror to pin back her hair, noticing the gray strands that multiply weekly along her temples. Age comes with experience much more than it does with time. She puts on her shoes and coat and takes all of her savings from a drawer beneath the old mirror. The money is enough to travel there, but she doesn't know if it is enough to get back home. She leaves a note for her parents and walks out the door.

VIII

There is a grin that spreads across the bird's beak as longing surfaces like a wave cascading out from Mateusz's Hamlet and into the theater. This is his final scene. He is lying on the stage floor, dying the first of one thousand public deaths. It is a small price to pay for receiving all the love in the world.

These are words that are understood even across the language barrier. She stands in the crowd feeling so much like a stranger, sensing the way that people look at her, for she is so obviously unlike everyone around, and yet somehow these people welcome her, because she is different, because she has come so far.

Why did she have to come? Why did she pack her bags, leave her things, everything, just to travel from New York to Poland and see for herself? She felt an emptiness created by the absence of stories, by the ones her parents did not tell. She lived with the isolation created by her mother's hysterics, her father hiding out alone in his library with his cigars, his books, his prayers, and his regrets. He never said anything to her, but she knew. Her mother was not his true love. Even though it was forever hidden, there was evidence of his story in his every action, his every word.

Her parents had left their whole world behind just so they could have a better life, but they did not have the chance to think about how this change, this deep sense of sadness and loss, would influence their children's future. Or maybe they only foresaw positive experiences, opportunity, happy times. How would their children learn to feel their roots when those connections had been so brutally severed?

IX

With a small blue glass memorial candle in hand, Anna boards the bus to Łódź. At first she feels nervous and shaky, eyes darting around, scanning her fellow passengers, as if there is someone to look for, somebody to tell, but within an hour the lull of the passing landscape calms her down. She wraps her light brown woolen coat around her neck, for even though it is spring, there is a strong chill in the air. The first promises of a colorful dawn give way to a gray, rainy day.

Her fellow travelers are joined together in this gloomy light. She watches them with interest. Beside her is an empty seat. Across the aisle sits a young mother with her daughter. The woman has long dark eyes and smooth alabaster skin, and she and her child eat sandwiches wrapped in a striped kitchen towel stuffed inside a simple cotton bag. At the front of the bus are two young priests, and at the back are three workers, all drunk, all sleeping. They are like a row of angry ducks leaning against the glass windowpane. Their snoring is intermittent, punctuated by moments of reprieve. The bus is otherwise empty, bumping along the road that leads Anna back home.

The Polish countryside passes with its little houses, its smoking chimneys, always burning, even now, in spring. Old ladies with patterned scarves on their heads, their faces so wrinkled you could read history in those lines, carry pails of fresh milk along the side of the road. Where are they going? They walk this way every day.

The world is bleak and heartbreaking, but it is also beautiful.

Anna closes her eyes and imagines what it will be like to step off the bus and set foot in Łódź once again. Her heart expands. Will there be anyone from the past to remember her face? Is there anything left standing inside the gates of the old school? Or is it just ashes? Just dust? *No matter, I will light my candle.* Anna's eyelids grow heavy, succumbing to sleep. She can already see herself turning the corner, just like she did for so many years. She approaches the imposing wrought iron gates, the old school building looming overhead. Inside the girls are waiting, their starched uniform dresses pressed, their shiny hair clean, their smiles radiant. Anna will open her hand and show them what she has been given. The gates will open. Something will begin.

X

You would never imagine this place as a stage set for a performance at dawn, but here it is, the gate outside Birkenau. Before you extends a great expanse of green and rows of empty bunkers. You ask yourself, why did you come?

When Mateusz climbs down from his place suspended above the crowd, he is still floating. It is not unusual for a performer to remain in the spotlight for long after the audience has gone. He carries the spotlight with him.

When Mateusz steps out into the night to light a cigarette, he sees that the audience has gathered. They are drinking, singing, building a bonfire. It is a strange sight, this merry crowd sitting at the edge of Birkenau, but this is the Polish landscape. Every space has a story to tell.

A tall figure walks toward him through the grass. It moves slowly, long white skirt gleaming in the night. Mateusz takes a drag from his cigarette and walks past the group to greet the figure. The light rain has lifted, and the fog is rolling in. His exhalation creates a stream of heat in the cool night air. Mesmerized as he nears the edge of darkness, he sees the woman from the audience, the one whom he imagined to be a mirage. He wishes to meet her, but as he gets closer he realizes that she is crying, her broad bony shoulders heaving uncontrollably as she looks out at the void, at the empty buildings so lonely and still in the quiet night. Mateusz stands there helplessly for several minutes, clearing from his throat a sudden unknown fear. He moves to face her. She is like no one he has ever seen. She is the most beautiful woman in the world, his wildest dream.

Different sounds converge, trying to emerge from his body, but he can only stumble. Finally he points to himself and says, "Mateusz," a murmur emitted from someone who has little practice making conversation. His introduction makes the woman smile. "Leah," she replies, and puts out her hand. In silence they walk back to the group, Leah looking out at the landscape, Mateusz watching her every move. He wants to ask her questions, find out if she can hear the haunting cry of this night, but he has no language with which to speak.

XI

The trip to eastern Poland is long, six hours to be exact. Though it is summer now, the weather has taken a turn for the worse, and a cold rain is beating down the road. The car Mateusz is driving was borrowed from a friend, and it lurches forward every so often, for he is new to shifting gears. He is new to driving as well, but he doesn't let on. Leah leans back against the stiff leather headrest of the tiny, canary yellow Fiat Maluch, her wild black hair spilling up toward the roof of the car. She watches the passing landscape, a constant rain of teardrops sliding down the window at her side. Yes, now she feels it. There is a great sadness bubbling up inside. *Who have I never met?* Leah wonders. *Who died? How many people did my parents mourn for? I can only look and wonder. I can never ask. I can never know. It would break their hearts to talk.*

Steam lifts from Mateusz's chest as he parks the car outside the town of N. He follows Leah as she walks up a faded path into the woods. It isn't far to walk before the first headstone, a matzevah, appears. This one is upright, like an obelisk, warning against intruders. And now the discovery begins. The dimensions of the old cemetery are not so big, but there are enough scattered gravestones left to inform passersby that Jews once lived here. Some matzevot are still standing but extremely faded. Others are practically buried beneath the earth, moss growing over their rough surfaces. Hebrew letters meet nature and dirt. Who wants to preserve this memory? Nothing can escape the weathering of time.

When she does finally discover her ancestor's grave, she is relieved to see that it has not been toppled, that it is still standing. Mateusz hangs back as Leah sits on a pile of wet leaves on the ground beside it. He can think only of how her long white skirt will be ruined, but he says nothing. Leah covers her face for a few minutes and murmurs something, though it is impossible for him to hear. When she rises and walks back to join him, she has an expression of strange bewilderment on her face and a different look in her eyes, almost as if she is accusing him of something. As they walk slowly back to the road, she stays off to the side. When they reach the car, Mateusz gets inside, but she remains standing, her back turned toward him, staring out at the open green field across the way. She climbs inside. Mateusz begins to drive. Leah opens her door and vomits outside of the moving car. Mateusz pulls over, offers her a handkerchief and some water, wishing to hold her in his arms. They drive through the woods for an hour in silence, the bumpy road knocking them about. She wonders if they will ever get out. At this moment the only thing Leah can think of is her bones.

When at last they emerge on the other side of the forest, they register at a small hotel near town.

As if an alarm clock goes off inside, Leah awakes just before dawn. Mateusz is still sitting in the same armchair where he sat the night before, as if waiting for this moment. Leah rises from the bed, naked, her pert breasts erect in the cold morning air, her long limbs graceful as she saunters to the window. She opens the curtains to reveal a view of the woods, tender with possibility in the early morning light. Everything is new. Life is predawn. She leans her back and buttocks against the window and stretches open her arms toward Mateusz. He runs. Right there, against the window, a crow screeching in the woods just beyond, these two foreigners, born on opposite sides of the same culture, making love into the early morning light.

XII

There is a melody played in that subtle twinkle of stars in the vast summer night. Anna moves between worlds as her eyelids become heavy and she dozes on the bus. Here the gray, rainy day, drunken men snoring at the back of the bus, the sweet child resting in her mother's arms, and rain drifting along the windowpane, like tears of nostalgia flying out of the past. With eyes closed she reaches the inside world, the one filled with night. The moon is full in the dream world. The school gates open: Anna walks inside. Rachelka descends the old crumbling staircase, running. Her hair is long and gray and wild, but she still wears her old school uniform. She extends her hand toward Anna and speaks with the same, childlike voice.

"*Kochana* (dear) Anna, we have been waiting for you all this time."

"I know," Anna replies. "I tried to come, but it took me so long." She hugs Rachelka and looks up to see all of their old classmates standing along the stairs, watching them.

"I have a candle for you," Anna says, handing the blue glass memorial candle to Rachelka. The glass is frosted from the heat of her hands.

Rachelka smiles. "To remember us by?" She reaches into her pocket and pulls out a small matchbox. "We can light it."

Rachelka lights the candle and places it on the ground.

Tears begin to pour down Anna's cheeks. She falls to the ground at Rachelka's feet. "Yes! Yes! To remember you by! I am sorry! I am so sorry!" She cries into the dark and luminous night, her tears falling deep into the grooves of the stone walkway. A strong wind picks up all of the dust in the old abandoned schoolyard.

One by one, all the stars begin to fall to the ground. There is a rain of light as the girls emerge from the building and spill out into the courtyard. In silence, they band together as stars cascade above their heads.

Anna ceases to cry. She stands there, mystified.

"Come on, let's run," Rachelka says, taking Anna by the hand.

And up they go. Those stairs that they have known for all of their lives now become a road to freedom. Forty-one Sarahs on their way home.

XIII

This bird has a map of the whole world engraved in its memory. It knows the best way to travel from South America to North, to reach the Holy Land, to travel from Kraków to Białystok. It knows all there is to know, as if it has lived everywhere and always, and through all time, which in fact it has. This bird saw the beginning. Watched clouds as they separated into dust, lands unhinge, and water as it collected into vessels built into the land. This bird was transformed from airborne white-feathered being to shadowed creature as it saw the commotion of separation, like two lovers saying goodbye, as light lifted from darkness, and sky from earth. Now there is a world. Now there is longing. Now there is a wound. Now there is intimacy experienced by the earth only through the extended rays of light, through the feet that wander, the animals that run, the grass that grows and heaves on the side of this mountain like a great wild bear breathing secretly with the rhythms of life that circle all around. This bird heard the first sounds emitted in the dark, the touch that brought stars down from the heavens, the one that brought man into a woman's arms. Then the bitter fruit.

The bus is traveling fast now, along a narrow road that connects one highway to the next. They call it a shortcut. There is a row of poplar trees on either side of the road, and they look so strong in that delicate wash of rain, as if no act of nature could wipe them away. Anna wants to stay awake, to view the passing countryside, to contemplate her past, her future, to remember the way to Łódź, but she is so tired that her head keeps dropping and she nods off to sleep.

She is in full slumber now, standing with the girls on the rooftop of her old school, stars everywhere around them, on their bodies and in their hair. She is so far removed from the reality of this journey by bus that she has no way to know that the driver, too, is succumbing to the sleepy mood of the day, his eyelids so heavy, his head caught every few minutes on its way down to his chest. He finds this extreme sleepiness alarming, and therefore accelerates his speed and opens the window, hoping that the fresh air and the swift movement will keep him awake.

But sleepiness is not the real problem. From out of nowhere the great bird arrives, black wings like an armed wrecking ball, come to test the boundaries of in-between. It crashes through the front windshield of the bus, sweeping wet shards of glass across the seats. Beyond awake now, the bus driver does what he can to keep a steady hand, but there is nothing to prevent him from moving toward those beautiful, strong, poplar trees. They will crush the bus to pieces. They are eternal, everlasting beings.

Anna feels a slight tug at her side that becomes stronger and stronger. She experiences a pain so deep and alarming that she is confused as to what is going on. She is awoken by her own muffled scream. A great trembling wing wraps around her. It seems to shield her from the blow. There is a beating heart at her side. There is also her own. One more moment and it will be over, she hears her own voice say, as if she is already separating from her body. *But, oh, the candle* . . . she thinks, and then the light of day.

XIV

A staircase rapidly forms above the rooftop of the old school as all the stars come together to pave the way for the girls' ascent. They walk up in single file, respectful of one another, still obedient. They look out at the vision of this new realm in awe. At last they are climbing out of death and into freedom. In the arms of the universe, they enter all time.

Rachelka hangs back on the roof watching them go one by one, for she feels responsible for them all. In the dream she needed a guardian to watch over her, but in truth she is the guardian, protector of all the other girls. She is the last Sarah to go.

Anna's tears turn to light as she witnesses this image. She begins to float, just a few centimeters off the ground, but it feels like ecstasy. Now Rachelka is helping little Sarah onto the staircase, encouraging her not to be afraid. She is next. She looks into Anna's eyes.

"Will you come with us?" she asks.

Anna lifts a bit higher.

"Not yet," Anna says. "I will go another way." And, with that, she kisses Rachelka and then opens her eyes.

Against pain, it is difficult to keep her eyes open, but somebody yells at her to stay awake, and so Anna does everything she can to obey. *I want to stay. I want to stay.* This is the mantra that keeps her on this plane. There is the strong smell of blood in the air, so potent that it almost transmits color. There is shouting, there is someone on the ground. They hold her hand. "Squeeze it," they say, and she does. "Very good, my dear."

The rain pours heavily now, and every tear that surfaces on Anna's face is swiftly wiped away, caught up in the current of life. A swooshing sound overhead calls to attention a large black bird that passes over the treetops and soars up, into the sky, through the rain. The bird looks down at her, eyes seen from far away. *I wonder if he is telling me something?* Anna asks herself. And the bird emits a loud, haunting sound.

Here there are no traveling lights, no stars on the ground. The pain is overwhelming, the senses, the sounds. *But I want to stay,* Anna hears her own voice say. *I love the world. I want to begin again.*

XV

There is a way to make love where you inch toward erasing the world, your home, your past. There is a way to feel something like God or heaven in those moments, because nothing on earth could ever be so beautiful.

He has dreamt of this, but it has never happened before. Never has the trembling of emotions traveled all the way through his body, to the very peripheries, and never before could he feel the reverberations inside somebody else's womb. This is what they call making love. And all he can think about is death. Thoughts come to him swiftly now, as if this pleasure is too much for any single human being to endure. *Will I die now? Will this climax take me into oblivion?* There is no one to ask. Her body has all the answers. He looks into her dark eyes, so filled with emotion as tears drop from the corners of her eyes. She screams with pleasure.

It is like nothing he has ever experienced, the large black bird that emerges from his chest and grows even bigger once outside, flying like a ghost body through the window and out into the morning light. It stops at a distant tree and turns back to look at him. Their eyes meet. The bird crows loudly and then disappears into the clouds. Now everything will change, and Mateusz will never know just what piece of him was lost as that great bird took flight.

This is the most extraordinary moment of his life. This is the instant where he falls deeply in love, the moment at which they create a child.

XVI

When the war had been over for less than a year and Mateusz was newly born, evenings were always peaceful on Ulica Strzelecka. When dinner was over Wiktor and Waleria retired to their room to listen to the radio and have a little drink, as they always did on Sunday nights. Bolesław was humming a tune with his surprisingly operatic baritone while whittling something in the kitchen for the baby. Elżbieta tiptoed into the darkened bedroom just to see the sleeping infant one more time. It was still hard to believe in his presence, that he was there, so pure, so sweet, so beautiful, so alive. She went over to his cradle and couldn't resist kissing him on the forehead, but she didn't wake him. He just stirred gently in his crib and smiled.

"*Kocham cie*," she whispered as she stepped away. I love you.

And as she reached the old brass knob on the heavy door, out of the corner of her eye she saw a great dark figure, like a bird, swoop over to the baby and disappear. Her heart sped up for a moment as she leapt over to the crib, worried that her hallucination had been real. Mateusz continued to sleep peacefully. She rubbed her eyes. *I must be tired,* she thought. *It's just a bit of fear, a bit of dust,* she assured herself, and then left to sit quietly with her parents as the night wore on. It was the spring of 1946, and everything felt so alive. The war was over. A new, happy life had just begun.

XVII

My parents, I have seen you. Will you hold me dear? Will you help me to step into the mysteries of life, one hand in the air, the other by your side? What will our language be? Our shared beliefs? You are two sides of the same coin, and in that dissonance there is so much history. What music will we make together? I have seen you and I want to ask you so many things, but already the time has come for me to begin.

This heart is so light that it needs the weight of gravity, of human form, to keep it down, to explore. It is evening, it is morning. We begin this way. Like shards of light sent from the original spark, we spread open the night. Yes, us, we come down into the light. And we hide from our own beauty.

XVIII

The swelling of the heart is like a call to prayer or a call to mourning. Sometimes the surging waves and the rocking of the boat make Wolf feel as if he is moving toward the end of the world. When overwhelmed by seasickness and sadness he closes his eyes and focuses on the image of Leah, his baby daughter's face. How he longs to see her again. She has a light within her that is unusually bright. Wolf feels that it is almost as if all of their ancestors have banded together to create the most beautiful life, as if she will live out all the highest destinies they had once imagined as their own. She is the spark.

ALSO FROM NEW EUROPE BOOKS

Ballpoint: A Tale of Genius and Grit, Perilous Times, and the Invention that Changed the Way We Write. 978-0-9825781-1-7

Eastern Europe!: Everything You Need to Know About the History (and More) of a Region that Shaped Our World and Still Does. 978-0-9850623-2-3
"A commendable feat."—*Library Journal*

The Devil Is a Black Dog: Stories from the Middle East and Beyond. 978-0-9900043-2-5
"A master class in how to tell a war story."—*Kirkus Reviews* (starred review)

The Essential Guide to Being Hungarian: 50 Facts & Facets of Nationhood. 978-0-9825781-0-0

The Essential Guide to Being Polish: 50 Facts & Facets of Nationhood. 978-0-9850623-0-9

Illegal Liaisons. 978-0-9850623-6-1

Keeping Bedlam at Bay in the Prague Café. 978-0-9825781-8-6

Once Upon a Yugoslavia. 978-0-9000043-4-9

Petra K and the Blackhearts. 978-0-9850623-8-5

The Wild Cats of Piran. 978-09900043-0-1

Voyage to Kazohinia. 978-0-9825781-2-4

New Europe Books

Williamstown, Massachusetts

Find our titles wherever books are sold,
or visit www.NewEuropeBooks.com for order information.